SEDUCED INTO HER BOSS'S SERVICE

BY

CATHY WILLIAMS

MILLS & BOON

First published in Great Britain 2016
By Mills & Boon, an imprint of HarperCollins*Publishers*
1 London Bridge Street, London, SE1 9GF

Large Print edition 2016

© 2016 Cathy Williams   **LP**

ISBN: 978-0-263-26218-6

Printed and bound in Great Britain
by CPI Antony Rowe, Chippenham, Wiltshire

CHAPTER ONE

'HE'S HERE!'

Sunny looked up from where she was buried in a mound of paperwork and reference books. The paperwork was to be filed, the reference books to be consulted for precedents on a complex tax issue which her boss was working on.

With a workload that barely gave her time to escape to the bathroom, she had still not been able to ignore the fever-pitch excitement that had gripped Marshall, Jones and Jones ever since they had learned that Stefano Gunn was going to be throwing some business their way.

Literally, Sunny had thought, *throwing business*, in much the same way as someone might throw a bone for a dog. Marshall, Jones and Jones was a recent addition to the legal scene in London. Yes, some really bright lights had been poached from a couple of the bigger firms but essentially it was still just a fledgling medium-sized firm without the decades of experience a man like Stefano Gunn would be looking for.

But he had *thrown some business* in their direction and speculation was rife.

Even lodged in the smallest honeycomb of rooms at the furthest end of the building, with her head firmly in her work and her body language projecting all sorts of *not interested in rumours* signs, rumours had still trickled down to her.

He had chosen their firm to handle some patent work for him because of Katherine, one of the partners. He fancied her and so he had chosen to sweeten her up by flinging a bit of work at them.

Sunny thought that that was a stupid piece of pointless speculation. Why on earth would the man do that? When he could make a simple call and ask for a simple date? Like any other normal person? Not, she knew, that Stefano Gunn was like any other normal person. Most normal people weren't capable of holding the city of London in the palm of their hand at the tender age of thirty-something.

Not that she was giving any of the fuss much thought. At the end of the day, all work was good work for a new company and the work he would be giving them might be peanuts for him but, for them, it would result in a hefty pay packet for the company.

Now, she propped her chin in her hand and looked at Alice, who shared the office with her.

Alice was small, plump, talkative and found it almost impossible to sit still for any period of time. Hence, out of all of the juniors who worked at this end of the building, she had been the one who had made it her duty to find out as much as she could about the billionaire.

For the past two weeks, she had carried every file and report from their offices to those of the bigwigs who occupied the other two floors of the building. Every time she had returned, she had brought with her more titbits of information Sunny had largely ignored.

'And did you manage to get a glimpse of The Big Man?' Sunny asked, eyebrows raised.

'Well...'

'Just a simple *yes* or *no*...'

'Don't be such a spoilsport, Sunny.' Undeterred, Alice dragged a chair over and positioned it directly in front of Sunny's desk. 'You can't be *that* uninterested!'

'I bet you I can be,' but she grinned back. Alice was everything Sunny had always imagined would get her back up. She spoke in just the sort of cut-glass accent Sunny had always found irritating and offensive, bounced around with the irrepressible self-confidence of someone for whom life had always been kind and, to top it off, had only got the job at the law firm because, as she freely admitted on day one, her father had connections.

But, mysteriously, Sunny had taken to her and so now, although she just wanted to get on with her work, she was willing to take a bit of time out to indulge her colleague.

'No,' Alice sighed and pouted. 'And I couldn't even quiz Ellie for details about him because everyone out there is on good behaviour. Anyone would think that she'd suddenly had a personality transplant. She's *always* happy to chit-chat…'

'Perhaps she just had a heavy workload,' Sunny said gently, 'and didn't think that ten-fifteen in the morning was the right time to settle down for a good gossip about a new client.'

'Not just *any old client*…'

'I know. We've all heard about the wondrous Stefano Gunn…'

'And you're really not impressed, are you?' Alice said curiously. 'How come?'

'I'm hard to impress.' Sunny was smiling but she had tensed up inside. She wondered when she would be cured of that, when she would be able to deal with personal questions without freezing up. Would she ever really be able to relax or was that something that would always be denied her? Alice hadn't been prying, hadn't actually asked her anything that could be called *personal* and yet Sunny had not been able to prevent that instinct to withdraw.

She knew she was buttoned up. She knew the group she worked with, who were all her age, found her pleasant enough but distant and unapproachable. She guessed they probably gossiped and speculated about her behind her back. She was the way she was and she knew why she was the way she was but she still couldn't change it and sometimes, like now, she wished she could.

She wished she could lean into Alice, who was gazing at her like a good-natured, eager little brown-eyed puppy, waiting for her to say something.

'Someone like that just isn't the type of guy… er…that I could ever find…well…I'm not impressed by someone because they're rich or good-looking…' she finished lamely, before gesturing to the pile of paperwork on her desk. 'It's good that he's going to be letting the company handle some of his business. I'm sure all the partners will be thrilled...but anyway...'

'Who gives a hoot about all the partners? If he's after Katherine, I think she'll be thrilled by more than just the business he's bringing to the company.' Alice grinned. 'I'll bet he'll be thrilling her over more than just a desk and a cappuccino...with Sammy sitting in the corner taking notes...I'll bet he'll be thrilling her in all sorts of different ways tonight when they celebrate the business he's given us without a bunch of prying office eyes on them... Although...' she ran a canny eye over Sunny and grinned '...if it's looks he's after, you're a hottie—if only you'd dress the part. And whoa! I'm going before you shoot me down in flames for saying that!'

She stood up briskly, still grinning as she brushed her short, short skirt and asked whether there was some paperwork she could take to the third floor. No? Well...she'd better be off and do a couple of minutes' work...

Sunny watched her saunter back to her desk but her mind was off her work now. As if a man like

Stefano Gunn would ever find her in the least bit attractive. Ridiculous.

Everyone had heard of Stefano Gunn. The whole world had heard of Stefano Gunn. Or at least anybody who was anybody and didn't live with their head buried in the sand. The man was ridiculously rich and stupidly good-looking. Not a day passed without his name popping up in the financial pages of a newspaper, reporting some deal or other he had secured which would boost his already inflated bank balance.

Sunny never read the tabloids but she was pretty sure that if she had she would have found him popping up there as well because ridiculously rich and stupidly good-looking men never led monk-like lives of self-restraint and solitude.

They led playboy lives with Barbie-doll women tripping along behind them and hanging on to their arms like limpets.

None of this was any of her concern, but Alice had opened up a train of thought which was normally kept safely locked away and, like opening a Pandora's box, Sunny could feel all those toxic thoughts uncurling from their dark corners and slithering through her head.

She stared at the computer winking at her and

at the dense report she had been instructed to read. What she saw was her own life staring back at her—the pathos of her childhood, the foster home and all that horror, the boarding school to which she had been given a scholarship and all those girls who had made it their duty to sideline her because she wasn't one of them.

Self-pity threatened to engulf her and she had to breathe deeply to clear her head, to focus on all the positives in her life now, all the chances she had grasped and the opportunities she had taken that had led her to this up-and-coming law firm where she could gain experience whilst completing her LPC.

Deep, deep, *deep* inside, she might carry those scars that could still cause her pain but she was twenty-four now and grown-up enough to know how to deal with that pain when it threatened to surface.

Like now.

The report swam back into focus and she lost herself in her work, only surfacing when her phone buzzed on the desk. Internal line. When she looked at her watch, she was startled to find that it was already twelve-thirty.

'Sunny!'

'Hi, Katherine.' In her head, Sunny pictured Katherine, one of the youngest full partners in any law firm in the city. She was tall, slim, with a sharp brown bob and open, intelligent brown eyes. Her impeccable background had primed her for a life of solid achievement and she had fulfilled all her potential. Every so often, she joined some of the other girls lower down the pecking order for drinks after work because, as she had once said, it didn't do to wedge yourself into an ivory tower and pretend that anyone who didn't live there with you didn't exist. So she would come out for a drink and, on one of those rare occasions when Sunny had actually been coerced into joining her colleagues, had confided that the only thing missing in her life was the husband and the kids, which she never tired telling her parents would never come. They just didn't believe her.

Katherine was a one hundred per cent career woman and Sunny's role model because, as far as Sunny was concerned, the only reliable thing in life was your career and, if you worked hard enough, it would never let you down. The letting down always came from people.

'I realise it's your lunch hour and I really do

hate to impose but I'm going to have to ask you to do me a small favour... Perhaps you could meet me in the conference room?'

'Is it to do with the files Phil Dixon asked me to go through? Because I'm afraid I'm not finished with them just yet...' And she'd been working flat-out but, unlike most of her other colleagues, she had debts to pay and the after-work job she held down left her precious little time to devote to work once she finally made it back to the flat she shared with Amy.

She heard anxiety creep into her voice. The files weren't due back for another week but she still tensed up in preparation for disappointment or a reprimand.

'Oh, no, nothing like that. Meet me in the conference room and of course bring whatever you're working on with you. And don't worry about lunch. I'll have whatever you want sent up to you.'

Inside, the building was cold, thanks to air conditioning. Outside, the sun was shining, the skies were blue and, as she walked up the two flights of stairs to the conference room, she noted that a lot of the offices were half empty.

St James's Park was only minutes away from

the building and, on a fine summer day, who would want to stay indoors and eat at their desk? Or even bring a sandwich back to their desk? Not many people.

She hit the third floor and immediately went into the plush cloakroom to neaten up.

The image that stared back at her was as tidy as it always was. Her long silvery-blonde hair, flyaway fine and, when loose, a riot of tumbling curls, was tightly pinned back into a chignon at the nape of her neck. Her white blouse was pristine, as was the grey knee-length skirt. There was no need to inspect her pumps because they would be shiny and unscuffed.

She was a businesswoman and she always left the flat every single morning having made sure that she looked the part.

The striking looks, which had never done her any good at all, were always ruthlessly played down. Occasionally she wished she had poor eyesight so that she could play them down even more with a pair of thick-rimmed glasses.

Alice had called her a *hottie* and she had flinched from the description because it was the last thing in the world she wanted to be seen as and she made strenuous efforts to make sure she wasn't.

Katherine was waiting for her in the conference room, a large space impeccably decorated in muted colours. Long walnut table which could seat twenty people around it, a matching sideboard to house coffee- and tea-making facilities, pale tan carpet and vertical blinds at the floor-to-ceiling windows. No bright colours, no demanding paintings, no eye-catching plants.

And next to Katherine was...

A small child mutinously sitting with her arms folded and a variety of gadgets next to her—iPad, iPhone, sleek, slim computer.

'Sunny, this is Flora...'

Flora didn't bother looking up but Sunny's mouth dropped open.

'I know you're probably surprised but I need to ask you to sit with Flora until my business with her father is over.' She mouthed something over the child's head that Sunny didn't understand and then eventually said, moving to stand next to Sunny and out of earshot, 'Her grandmother was supposed to be looking after her but she's been called away and dropped her off half an hour ago.'

'I'm babysitting?' Sunny was appalled. She had never been one of those girls with a driving maternal instinct. She'd had no experience to speak of with kids and the little she did have had not left her with glorious rosy memories. The kids she had met at the school she had attended off and on until the age of ten had been horrible. Even then she had been a victim of bullying by most in her peer group because of the way she looked—blonde-haired, green-eyed with, she had overheard one parent telling another with just a hint of malice, the face of an angel. At an age where the most important thing was to blend in, she had stuck out like an elephant in a china shop and had paid the price.

Life lessons had taught her that the safest route to follow was the most invisible one and being highly visible had not drawn a vast circle of friends around her.

She'd never babysat for anyone. She had grown up fast. There had been no room in her life for playing games and especially not playing games with young children.

What on earth was she supposed to do with this one?

'She's hardly a baby, Sunny,' Katherine corrected with a smile. 'And you really won't have to do anything, which is why I told you to bring whatever you're working on with you. It's comfortable here and I've booked you in for the afternoon. I should be wrapped up with Mr Gunn by around five-thirty.'

'This is *his* child?' Sunny's jaw hit the ground with a thud and Katherine grinned.

'Unless he's having us on and, trust me, he's not the sort to have anyone on. We're not exactly rolling in the aisles from his sense of humour in there.'

'So…!' She stepped briskly back towards the child, who eventually looked up when there was no choice because Katherine had made introductions and was heading at speed towards the door.

Sunny got the feeling that the other woman was probably as awkward around young kids as she was.

The door shut and Sunny walked towards Flora and looked at her for a few seconds without saying anything.

She was a beautiful child. Long dark hair flowed down her back; her eyelashes were so long they brushed her cheeks, the eyes staring right back at her were huge, almond-shaped and as dark as night.

'I don't want to be here either.' Flora scowled and folded her arms. 'It's not my fault Nana had to drop me off.'

A surly, rebellious child was more what Sunny felt she could deal with and she breathed a quiet sigh of relief. 'You've brought all your toys to play with?' She eyed the collection of high-end gadgets and wondered how many other children of eight or nine walked around with thousands of pounds' worth of electronics to amuse them.

Faced with this unexpected job, she had had no time to ponder over the weird fact that the billionaire Stefano Gunn had a child. He might feature in the *Financial Times* with the regularity of a subscription holder but she had to concede that he was very private when it came to his personal life because, as far as she knew, no one was aware of the fact that he had a daughter.

For that she owed him more credit than she had otherwise thought.

'I'm bored with them.' Flora yawned extravagantly without putting her hands over her mouth.

'How old are you?'

'Why do you want to know?'

'You may think you're tough but you can never outdo me when it comes to being tough,' Sunny said honestly, which provoked a fleeting spark of interest. 'How old are you?'

'Nearly nine.'

'Good.' She beamed and walked towards the files she had lugged into the room with her. 'In that case, if you're bored with your toys you can help me with my work...'

Long legs stretched out at an angle, Stefano did his utmost to stifle a yawn.

This entire situation could have been handled by one of his employees. In fact, had it not been for his mother, this entire situation would not have been happening in the first place.

He had a perfectly competent team of in-house lawyers and had they not been up to the job of dealing with this particular slice of intricate patent law then he would have immediately gone to the biggest and the best.

Instead, here he was, at his mother's instigation, sitting in the offices of a company that was so new that it had barely left the embryo stage.

'Jane's daughter works there. You remember my friend Jane, don't you?'

No, he didn't. With those opening words three weeks ago, Stefano had been able to second-guess where his mother was going and Jane's daughter, whoever she was, was going to feature in the scenario.

It wasn't the first time Angela Gunn had tried to set him up. Ever since his ex-wife had died, driving too fast, having had too much to drink in a car that was way too sporty for winding New Zealand back roads, his mother had been keen to find him a suitable woman who could provide, as she was fond of telling him, a stable, nurturing maternal influence in his daughter's life.

'A girl needs her mother,' she had repeatedly said in a wistful voice. 'Flora barely knows you and she misses Alicia…that's why she's finding it so hard to adjust…'

Stefano had had to agree with his mother on at least one count and that was that he barely knew his daughter, although he always made sure to refrain from telling his mother just why that was the case.

His marriage to Alicia had been brief and disastrous. Having met young, what should have been no more than a passing fling had turned into a marriage of necessity when she had fallen pregnant. On purpose? That was a question he had never directly asked, but was there really any need? Alicia had come from New Zealand to study and had decided to stay on to work in one of the larger London hospitals as a nurse. He had met her there when he had suffered three broken ribs while playing rugby and the rest, he had always thought, was history. He had lusted after her, she had played coy and hard to get and then, when he had eventually got her into bed, safe in the knowledge that she was taking the Pill and, as a nurse, would be only too aware of the importance of making sure she stuck to the rigid regime, she had *had an accident.*

'I remember having a tummy upset,' she had told him, winding her arms around his neck and snuggling against him while he felt the bottom of his world drop away, 'and I don't know if you know but sometimes, if you have a stomach bug, the Pill doesn't work…'

He had married her. He had walked up the aisle with all the enthusiasm of a man walking to meet his executioner. They hadn't been married for five minutes before he realised the enormity of his mistake. Alicia had changed overnight. With free rein to more money than she could ever know in a lifetime, she had taken to spending with an exuberance that bordered frenetic. She had begun demanding that he spend more time with her. She had complained incessantly about the hours he worked and thrown hissy fits if he was late back by more than two minutes.

He had gritted his teeth and told himself that pregnancy hormones were to blame, even though he knew that they weren't.

When Flora was born, her demands had become more insistent. She needed constant, round the clock attention. Their London mansion became a battleground and the less he wanted to return to it, the more spiteful she became in her verbal attacks.

And then she began, as she took great pleasure in telling him, to *find stuff to do because she was bored and he was never around.*

He found out what that *stuff* was when he returned to the house early one afternoon and caught her in bed with another man. The fact that he had not felt a shred of jealousy had been the clearest indication that he needed a divorce.

What should have been a straightforward separation of ways, for he had been more than willing to give in to her strident, excessive demands for the sake of his daughter, had turned into a six-year nightmare. She had grabbed the money on the table and fled back to New Zealand, from where she had imperiously controlled his visiting rights, which, from the other side of the world, had been difficult, to say the least.

He had done his utmost to fight her for more reasonable custody but it had been impossible. She had thwarted him in every way conceivable and only her premature death had granted him the child he had fought so hard to know, but in reality had only seen a handful of times.

Now he had Flora but the years had returned him a daughter he didn't know, a daughter who resented him, who was sullen and uncooperative.

A daughter who, having now lived with him for nearly a year, *needed*, as his mother kept insisting, *a mother figure*.

He looked at Katherine Kerr, who was frowning at the various company accounts he had brought with him.

'You mustn't worry about your daughter.' She caught his eye and smiled warmly. 'I've left her in the capable hands of one of our brightest stars.'

Katherine Kerr was intelligent, attractive and empathetic. His mother would be hoping that they would click, that his next step would be to ask her out to dinner. It wasn't going to happen.

'I'm not worried about Flora,' he drawled. 'I'm worried that if we don't put this one to bed soon I'm going to miss my five-thirty meeting at the Savoy Grill.'

'It all looks fairly straightforward.' Katherine closed the file and sat back. 'If you're happy to leave it with us, then I can assure you we'll do an excellent job for you, Mr Gunn.'

Stefano looked at his watch and stood up. If the woman was looking for things to go further, then she was going to be disappointed. 'If you tell me where I can find my daughter, Miss Kerr, then I won't keep you any longer. I take it you now have all the relevant information you need to proceed with this patent case?'

Yes, she did. Yes, it was a pleasure doing business with him. She hoped that should he need any further legal work, he would consider their firm.

Leaving the office, Stefano decided that he would have to gently tell his mother that she would have to curb her desire to find him a wife. It wasn't going to happen. She would have to accept that when it came to women, he liked things just the way they were. Pretty, undemanding and admittedly not over-bright little things who came and went and allowed him windows of fun and sex for as long as he required them. It worked.

He made his way to the conference room, already bracing himself for the expected confrontation with his daughter and feeling mightily sorry for whoever had had the dubious pleasure of looking after her. Flora had a special talent for making her antagonism known and she was invariably antagonistic towards anyone babysitting her.

The offices smelt of recently applied paint and newly acquired carpet and had been decorated in just the sort of style he liked, which was understated and unpretentious.

This wouldn't have been a natural choice for him when it came to law firms but he'd liked what he'd seen and he was toying with the idea of throwing some more work their way as he knocked perfunctorily on the door before pushing it open and striding into the room.

Sunny looked up.

For a few seconds she felt winded, as though the breath had been knocked out of her.

She knew what Stefano Gunn looked like. Or at least she'd *thought* she'd known. She'd seen blurry pictures of him in the financial pages of the broadsheets, shaking hands, looking satisfied at some incredible deal he'd just pulled off. A tall, good-looking man whose roots lay in Scotland but whose looks were far from Scottish.

Seeing him in the flesh was a completely different matter. He wasn't just *good-looking*. He was staggeringly, sinfully *sexy*.

He was very tall, his body lithe and muscular under the hand-tailored suit. His black hair was slightly long, curling at the nape of his neck, and the arrangement of his features...was dramatic. Everything about him oozed exotic sex appeal and she found that she was holding her breath.

Horrified to be caught staring, she pulled herself together at speed and stood up, hand automatically outstretched.

'Mr Gunn. I'm Sunny Porter...'

His cool fingers as they briefly touched her sent an electric impulse racing through her body and when she withdrew her hand she had to fight not to wipe it on her skirt.

'Flora...' she turned to the child, who hadn't glanced up and was ferociously highlighting the photocopied piece of printed paper which Sunny had given her '...your father's here.'

'Flora!' Stefano's tone was sharp but he modulated it to add, 'It's time to go.'

'I'd rather stay here,' Flora said coolly, throwing Stefano a challenging stare.

For a few terse seconds complete silence greeted this mutinous remark. Embarrassed, Sunny cleared her throat and began shuffling her papers together. She could feel his presence and it was suffocating.

'You seem to have captured my daughter's interest with...what exactly is she doing?'

Sunny reluctantly looked up. She was tall, at five eight, but she still had to crane her neck to meet his eyes.

She's beautiful was the thought that sprang into Stefano's head as he stared down at her. Not just pretty or attractive, but a stunner, even though she couldn't have done more to try and conceal that fact.

Her clothes were cheap and drab, the colours draining, but they still couldn't subdue the radiant, startling beauty of her heart-shaped face and those huge green eyes. His gaze roamed the contours of her face, taking in the small straight nose and the full, perfectly formed mouth.

Sunny was used to men staring but Stefano's

brooding dark eyes didn't send her irritation levels soaring. Instead, she felt her nipples pinch with sudden, forceful awareness and an unfamiliar, horrifying and unwelcome dampness spread uncomfortably between her legs.

Her response confused and panicked her.

Having lived the unstable, disjointed and bewildering life of a child with a mother whose primary concerns were men, drugs and drink, a mother who had been prone to disappearing for days on end, leaving her with a neighbour, any neighbour, Sunny prided herself on being tough, on being able to handle any situation.

Especially men.

She'd been attracting their attention since the minute she had become a teenager and started to develop. When her mother had died from an overdose, leaving behind her eleven-year-old daughter, she had been fostered by a couple and had lived on her nerves, uncomfortable with her foster father's leering eyes, terrified into locking her bedroom door every night although he'd stared but never touched.

At thirteen she had won a scholarship to an exclusive boarding school and, even there, she had been ostracised because of her remarkable looks. She was the cuckoo in the nest, out of her depth with girls who came from serious money, isolated because whenever boys happened to be around, they drooled over her.

She had hated every second of it all but the shell she had developed had protected her, had allowed her to ignore what couldn't be changed.

Men were driven to look at her. She had learned to blank them out.

She had told herself that the guy for her would be one who would want her for her brain, for what she had to say, for her personality.

Except when, at university, that guy had come along, dear, sweet John, who had been kind and chivalrous and thoughtful; she just hadn't been able to respond physically to him. That had been two years ago but it still hurt to think about it.

Had she, under the tough shell, been secretly searching for love? Had she longed for someone to ignite the sort of gentle romance she'd fantasised about in the deepest, darkest corners of her mind? Was that what had driven her to John, who had ticked all the right boxes as candidate for the Big Romance? If that had been the case, then she'd been way off mark and what she'd got hadn't been a Big Romance, but yet another tough learning curve which had closed the doors, for good, on any stupid belief that she was destined for a happy-ever-after life with the perfect soulmate. John should have been the perfect soulmate and she should have wanted to touch him all the time. It hadn't been that way at all. She'd concluded what she should have concluded a long time ago, which was that her background had irretrievably damaged her. She had moved on and accepted her lot.

So why was she all hot and bothered now? In the presence of a man like Stefano Gunn? Since when had she ever felt hot and bothered when some guy stared at her? Hadn't she stopped being an idiot two years ago when she and John had ended their doomed relationship?

'Flora didn't want to play with…any of her expensive toys—' she fought to remember that this was a very important client and swallowed down her natural instinct to be contemptuous '—so I gave her some work to do and she's been doing it for the past three hours.'

'Work?' He drew her aside while Flora continued doing what she was doing with the highlighters and making a pointed show of disinterest in his arrival.

'Not actual work,' Sunny explained, shifting a few inches away from him in an attempt to ward off the disconcerting impact of his presence. 'I photocopied some pages of one of my law books, Petersen versus Shaw, and asked her to read it and highlight the bits she thought were relevant to Petersen winning the case.'

'You did...*what*?'

'My apologies, Mr Gunn.' She stiffened, automatically defensive. What else was she supposed to do? Magic up some Lego and play building games with her? Was that even what eight-year-old girls were interested in doing? 'She said she was bored with whatever...games are on her iPad...or laptop...and I had a stack of work to get through...'

'I'm not criticising you,' Stefano said drily. 'I'm expressing open-mouthed amazement that Flora was drawn into doing something like that.'

Sunny relaxed and stole a glance at his handsome face. His voice was deep and lazy, as velvety as the smoothest of chocolate and his bronzed colouring spoke of an exotically foreign gene pool. And she could *breathe* him in, a woody, clean, utterly masculine scent that made her senses swirl.

'She's more than welcome to take the little file back with her.' She could feel the hot burn of an uncustomary blush. 'It's a historic case. I would never have given her anything that could have remotely been seen as sensitive information.'

'What are you doing later?'

'I beg your pardon?' Her eyes flew to his face in consternation.

'Later. What are you doing?' The Savoy Grill would have to be put on hold. 'I'd like to thank you for your impromptu babysitting by taking you out to dinner.'

'There's no need!' Sunny was aghast at the thought of having dinner with him. She was aghast at the thought of doing anything with the man, aside from saying goodbye and never clapping eyes on him again. He did something to her that she didn't like—something that made mincemeat of her nervous system—and for someone who valued her control that was tantamount to disastrous.

Stefano eyed her narrowly, taken aback by her horrified refusal.

'I...I couldn't.' She backtracked from being outright rude. 'I...happen to have a job that starts at six so I couldn't possibly…and there's really no need to thank me… All in a day's work…'

'A job?' He frowned. 'What job?'

'I…I work four nights in a restaurant… Qualifying to be a lawyer costs money, Mr Gunn,' she said bluntly. 'I also have rent to pay and food to buy. What I earn here doesn't quite stretch to cover it all.'

'In which case,' Stefano said smoothly, 'have dinner with me. I have a proposition for you and I think you'll find it…irresistible…'

CHAPTER TWO

SUNNY BARELY HAD time to make it home, change quickly and head out to the restaurant, which was just five minutes from where she lived and attracted an eclectic crowd of tourists and students because it was cheap, which appealed to the students, and trendy, which appealed to the tourists.

She had been lucky to get the job. The tips might not have been great because students were notoriously stingy when it came to that sort of thing, but the pay was better than average and the young couple who owned the place were generous, which meant that at the end of the week, if the takings had been particularly high, the staff were all given a small bonus over and above what they were paid.

Every penny went into Sunny's savings.

She was out of breath by the time she flew into the kitchen to change at speed out of her jeans and T-shirt and into the uniform, which was a jazzy red number, trousers and a T-shirt with the restaurant logo printed in bold white across the front, and a cap. Sunny had no idea what the significance of the outfit was and neither did Tom and Claire. They had decided on it because, Claire had confided, giggling, it had been a cheap bulk buy and the punters had seemed to like it so they had stuck with it.

'It's going to be a busy one tonight...' Claire was rushed off her feet. Tom was supervising in the kitchens, barking orders at the staff, and the other two waitresses were already zooming in and out, pinning orders to the cork board in the kitchen.

'I'm sorry I'm late,' Sunny apologised, stuffing her hair into the cap. 'I got held up at work.'

'No matter, darling. Go, go...go! Tom's having a meltdown because the tuna delivery hasn't arrived yet. You don't want to get anywhere near him!'

The trickle of customers was fast becoming a flood and Sunny went into autodrive. She had been working at TWC Eaterie for eight months and she knew the ropes. Take orders, smile a lot, race between kitchen and tables, deliver the orders and as soon as one set of diners had finished eating, get the bill to them as fast as she could so that the table could be cleared, making way for another lot to sit down. Sometimes, if the customers seemed to be dawdling a little too much over their coffees, Claire would turn up the volume on the music, just a notch, and that always seemed to remind them that it was time to go.

Sunny had her patch and she could work the tables blindfold. She chatted without really noticing who she was chatting to and she always added a smiley face to the bill when she brought it because she had read somewhere that it encouraged diners to leave bigger tips than they normally would.

This evening, she was particularly oblivious to the crowd. She'd thought of nothing but Stefano on the Tube ride back and he was still in her head as she dashed around the restaurant, distracting her, which got on her nerves.

The man had got under her skin.

Was it because he was just so good-looking? And why should that have made a difference anyway? Sunny had never been susceptible to good-looking men. She'd been chased by enough of them and heard enough of their corny lines to know that they were usually full of themselves and arrogantly all too aware of the effect they had on the opposite sex.

So why had Stefano Gunn proved the exception? Especially when she had given up on men? If she hadn't been able to feel any sort of physical attraction to a guy who had been perfect, then there was no hope for her. She had reconciled herself to that fact. She had assumed that she was frigid, a consequence of her turbulent background and a mother who had set a poor example when it came to self-restraint and decorum.

She touched the locket she wore around her neck. In it was one of only a handful of pictures she had of her damaged parent. Annie Porter might have been a terrible mother but there was still a big place in Sunny's heart for her. She felt that that must be what unconditional love was all about. Her mother would be the only recipient of that sort of love as far as Sunny was concerned. If she ever loved anyone again, and she wasn't even sure that she had loved John nearly as much as he had loved her, then there would be so many conditions that the weight of them would probably kill off any relationship before it could get going. Suited her.

But she hadn't had a relationship with anyone

since John and she wondered whether the effect Stefano had had on her had been a timely reminder that she was still young.

It made no difference anyway. She wasn't going to see him again. She had politely turned down his offer for dinner and had shown no interest in whatever proposition he had for her that she might find irresistible.

Dinner and a proposition could only add up to one thing as far as Sunny was concerned.

Bed.

Perhaps he saw her as a possible easy conquest. He was staggeringly rich and staggeringly good-looking and maybe he thought that if he made a pass at her, she wouldn't be able to resist. Maybe he thought that, as a relative junior in the company, she would be awestruck and open-mouthed and breathless with girlish excitement if he so much as glanced in her direction.

Maybe…no, *almost certainly*, that was where the *irresistible* aspect of his so-called offer came in.

She was so wrapped up in thoughts that she wanted to box away that she was convinced her mind was playing tricks on her when, with the crowd finally and thankfully beginning to thin out, she heard the sound of his dark, velvety voice behind her.

She spun round, only just managing to hang on to the tray she was balancing and stared.

It was a little after ten and he looked as bright-eyed and bushy-tailed as when she had last seen him at five-thirty, although he was no longer wearing his suit.

The suit had been replaced by a pair of black jeans and a fitted black jumper that did remarkable things for his lean, muscular build.

She couldn't find a thing to say. She actually blinked several times to make sure that she wasn't seeing things, that her mind hadn't conjured up his image because she had been thinking so much about him.

'So this is where you work...'

Sunny was galvanised into movement. 'What are you doing here, Mr Gunn?' She wasn't in the office now and she didn't see why she should try and modulate her voice to accommodate him. She stared at his face but she was aware of every part of him with every pore in her body. 'Look, I can't stop to chat to you.' She turned round abruptly and began heading towards the kitchen, heart beating like a sledgehammer inside her.

Fi, one of the girls who worked the tables with her, the only full-time waitress among them and a bubbly brunette who specialised in having boyfriend problems, was taking a little time out to catch her breath because her stint was almost over. Sunny was very tempted to ask her whether Stefano was still outside and, if he was, whether she could take his order but then she knew that that would lead to endless curiosity and, as always, the part of her that clammed up at the thought of confiding slammed into gear.

Maybe he would get the message and leave. Maybe he'd already left. Her hands were clammy and she wiped them on her trousers as she headed back out to the restaurant, which was now practically empty.

There was no avoiding or ignoring him. His presence was so powerful that it would have been impossible to overlook him even though he was sitting right at the back. He had pushed his chair at an angle so that he could stretch out his long legs and he looked utterly composed and relaxed.

Stifling a sigh of frustration, Sunny walked towards him, taking her time.

'I'm afraid we've already taken last orders,' she

said ungraciously, 'so if you've come here expecting a meal, then you're going to be disappointed.'

'Oh, dear. And the menu looked so interesting. Perhaps another day. However, that being the case, I'm assuming you'll be leaving shortly?'

'How did you even find out where I worked?' She looked at him with great reluctance and was assailed by the same unwelcome heady discomfiture she had felt before. His eyes were as dark as night and as captivating as an open flame to a moth. There was nothing safe or comforting about him but he had the sort of face she felt driven to stare at and the sort of compelling personality that wanted to suck her in and she had no intention of being sucked in.

Her memories of her mother were scattered but she remembered enough. She remembered how pretty her mother had been and how helpless she had been at the hands of men who had taken advantage of her. The roller-coaster ride that had been her childhood had built in her a capacity for self-control she never relinquished and a determination never to find herself in any situation with anyone that made her feel helpless. John had never made her feel helpless.

But something about Stefano Gunn made her feel helpless.

'Sit.'

Sunny folded her arms and stared at him. 'We're not in an office now, Mr Gunn...'

'Stefano, please.'

She chose to ignore that interruption. 'So I feel it's okay for me to be direct with you.'

'I've always encouraged directness in other people,' Stefano murmured. She was even more eye-catching than he remembered, even though the hair, he noted, was still tucked away and she wore no make-up.

She'd turned down his offer for dinner and rejected what he had to say without bothering to give him a hearing. She'd been pointedly polite about it but she hadn't been able to get away from him fast enough.

He was accustomed to women bending over backwards to attract his attention. He'd never been in the position of being with a woman who so clearly couldn't wait to escape his presence and he hadn't known whether to be irritated or amused by that.

'I don't know how you managed to find out where I work...'

'Not that difficult. I got your address from Katherine, went to your house, spoke to the girl who shares your flat with you, who told me where you worked and here I am.'

'You *spoke to Katherine*?' Sunny was outraged. She glanced round to see Claire looking at her curiously. 'I have to finish clearing the tables,' she muttered.

'I'll wait until you're finished and walk you home.'

'I don't need an escort, Mr Gunn.'

'I told you, the name is Stefano.' An edge of impatience had crept into his voice. Her simmering hostility and mutinous stubbornness, rather than putting him off, was goading him into digging his heels in. He'd come here to talk to her and talk to her he would. Maybe if it hadn't been for Flora, he would have shrugged off her cool refusal to listen to him although a little voice in his head was telling him that she posed a challenge and a challenge was something he had not experienced in a very long time.

Sunny didn't bother to answer. She knew she was attracting interested looks from her friends in the restaurant and that in itself made her bristle with annoyance at him.

How dared he track her down like this?

How dared he think that he could stampede over her very clear refusal to listen to his *proposition*?

How dared he think he could try and sweet-talk her into bed because he was filthy rich and she was just an ordinary junior in a law firm and therefore open to persuasion?

And how *dared* he compromise her position in the company by talking to her boss about her?

Rage bubbled up inside her as she raced through the remainder of her chores, wiping the tables and then, finally, changing back into her jeans and T-shirt and the denim jacket she had brought along because it was now quite cool outside.

'He's still there, you know,' Claire said, lounging by the kitchen door with a tea towel slung over her shoulder. She and Tom would stay on for at least another hour and in the morning they would count the takings. It had been a very good night. 'I know you've made a point of pretending not to notice, but he hasn't gone.'

Sunny flushed and scowled.

'My darling, none of us can miss the way the guys who come in here stare at you. I don't mean to intrude…I know you're a very private person, but haven't you ever been tempted to…to…?'

'Never,' Sunny said fiercely. 'I don't go for guys who are drawn to me because of the way I look.' She remembered her foster father's lecherous eyes following her through the house, while his invalid wife remained cheerfully oblivious, and shuddered.

'Who's your latest admirer?'

Sunny sighed and looked at Claire. 'He's not an admirer,' she admitted. Although why else would he be here? If not to try and get her into bed? She wasn't vain but she was realistic and being realistic protected her against having her head turned by meaningless, pretty words. 'Don't worry. I'll get rid of him and I'll make sure he doesn't come here again.'

Claire laughed. 'He looks rich. He can come whenever he wants, just as long as he puts his hand in his pocket and actually shows up in time to order food and drink!'

'I'll pass that on.' Sunny smiled weakly. She had no intention of doing any such thing. What she intended to do was find out just what he had said to Katherine and whether he had compromised her position in the company.

And she would have to do that without letting her temper explode. She would have to be cool, calm and collected whilst leaving him in no doubt that she wasn't interested in whatever he had to say to her.

She emerged and Stefano was almost surprised because he had half expected her to have disappeared through a back door. But there she was, in jeans and a T-shirt and, without the cap, her hair was long. Very long. Every shade of blonde feathering in curls down her back, although that didn't last very long because, even as she walked towards him, she was stuffing it into a ponytail.

She had the long, slender body of a ballet dancer and her movements were graceful. She was scowling, but not even the scowl could hide that startling, unusual prettiness. When she had been created, some small added ingredient had been thrown into the mix, elevating her from good-looking to unbelievably striking. Her green eyes were narrowed suspiciously on him as she finally came to a stop directly in front of him.

'I want to know what you said to Katherine.'

'You're not, are you?' Stefano stood up, towering over her, and she automatically fell back a step or two.

'Not what?'

'Sunny.' He shoved his hands in his pockets as they headed to the door. 'Your mother must rue the day she named you that. Unless, of course...' he pushed open the restaurant door, allowing her to brush past him '...you're sunny with everyone else but reserve all your bulldog belligerence for me...is that it? And, if so, why?'

'My mother died when I was a child,' Sunny said coldly. 'What did you tell Katherine?' She didn't want him walking next to her...didn't want him escorting her the short distance to her flat, but she felt as if she had no choice.

'I told her that I wanted to discuss something with you of a personal nature and she was kind enough to provide me with your address.'

'How dare you?' She rounded on him, hands on her hips, so furious that she felt she might explode. 'Do you have any idea how important that job is to me?' A series of scenarios ran through her head, each worse than the one before. He had put poor Katherine in a position...he was so important that she had had no choice but to do as he had asked...but in the morning, she, Sunny, would be called in for a little chat...she would be told that fraternising with clients was frowned upon…she would be warned…she might even be sacked… She hadn't been there very long and the last thing the company would want would be a lawyer who couldn't be trusted around clients… she would lose her job, her career and everything that made sense of her life…

And it would all be this man's fault.

'I don't want anything to do with you and how dare you tell my boss that you want my address? So that you can try and *come on to me*? How *dare* you?' Tears of anger and frustration were pricking the back of her eyes.

With just the street lights for illumination, his face was all angles and shadows. He towered over her and she couldn't read the expression on his face.

Just in case he hadn't got the drift, though, she thought that she should make herself perfectly clear.

'I'm not going to sleep with you, Mr Gunn, and I don't want you *pestering* me. I don't care how rich or powerful you are or how much business you're going to bring to the firm…*I* don't come as part of what's on offer to you!'

Stefano was genuinely outraged that she had

pigeonholed him as desperate and downright stupid enough to think about making a pass at her.

'Aren't you getting a little ahead of yourself?' he asked coolly.

That threw her and for a few seconds she stared at him in sudden confusion.

'Anyway, I hope I've made myself clear,' she muttered, dragging her eyes away from him and walking briskly towards the flat. He kept pace with her.

The flat she shared with Amy was cheap and thus located in a fairly dodgy part of town. A hop and a skip away, smart restaurants and trendy cafés lined the high street but here all of that gave way to rundown houses that were mostly let to people who couldn't afford anything better, and a couple of off licences and corner shops that stayed open beyond the call of duty.

'So—' she stopped in front of the door that led up to the flat she shared at the top of the converted Victorian house '—I'd appreciate it if you just left me alone, and please don't discuss me with my boss. It could jeopardise my position in the company.'

'Like I said…you're getting ahead of yourself here. I think you're confusing me with the sort of sad loser who's into pursuing reluctant women and can't take no for an answer.'

Sunny stared at him in silence, slowly realising that she had misunderstood the situation.

Mortification swept over her in a hot, burning tide. 'You said you had a proposition for me...' she stammered, so taken aback that she was barely aware of him removing the key from her hand, opening the door and urging her inside.

He shouldn't be coming in. He definitely *should not* be coming in. Amy wasn't going to be there. She was on nights and wouldn't be back until the following morning and Sunny couldn't imagine him being in the flat with her, just the two of them.

Although he wasn't *interested in her*, was he? When you thought about it, why the heck would he be? He could have any woman he wanted. He would just have to snap his fingers! She was so embarrassed at jumping to erroneous conclusions that she would happily have stepped into the hole if the ground had opened up beneath her feet.

While this jumble of thoughts was chaotically running through her head, they took the stairs and he let them into the flat with the key, which she had failed to take from him.

It was a very small two-bedroom flat with barely room to swing a cat. The décor was shabby and the furniture looked as though it had mostly been reclaimed from a skip somewhere. Not even the cheerful prints Blu-tacked to the walls could lift the place into something more cheerful. But it worked for both of them. They got along very well and, because Amy worked nights most of the month, they tended to see one another only in passing.

Looking around him, Stefano realised that he had never been anywhere like this before in his life. He knew that by anyone's standards his life had been one of unsurpassed privilege. The only child of a wealthy Scottish landowner and an Italian mother who, herself, had inherited a tidy sum of money when her parents had passed away, he had never had any occasion to find himself slumming it. Alicia, of course, had not had money but he had rarely ventured into the quarters she shared with her friends.

Here, amidst this drab, unappealing *ordinariness*, Sunny was the equivalent of an orchid in a patch of weeds. He could almost understand why she had misinterpreted his intentions, although that did nothing to detract from the umbrage he felt.

Although, a little voice whispered in his head, hadn't he looked at her with sexual interest? It wasn't going to happen.

Stefano swept that unwanted thought aside as fast as it had come.

'My daughter liked you,' he said without preamble.

'Did she? I have no idea why. I gave her work to do and I don't suppose many eight-year-olds would have appreciated that.' But she felt a rare bloom of pleasure at his words.

Released from the discomfort of thinking that he was just someone else attracted to her because of the way she looked, Sunny knew that she should be able to relax, but she was still as tense as a piece of elastic stretched to breaking point. He had sprawled out on one of the chairs in the tiny sitting room and he was just so wildly exotic that she could scarcely look at him without her breath catching in her throat and a weird tension invading her body.

'I had to bring Flora in with me because she managed to successfully see off the last nanny and my mother had to go unexpectedly to Scotland...'

'Oh.' Where was this going? Sunny was bewildered. 'When you say *see off the last nanny...*' This for no other reason than to fill the silence.

'Flora enjoys making life as difficult for her nannies as she humanly can.' Stefano sighed and raked his fingers through his hair.

'I don't see what this has to do with me.' His wife wasn't around. He was an eligible bachelor. The office gossip mill had made that perfectly clear from day one, when speculation had been rife that he was only handing them business because of Katherine. She perched on the edge of a chair and looked at him steadily.

'My mother will be up in Scotland for the next month. I have a nanny to cover for Flora during the day, as she's on holidays, but not even the most long-suffering of nannies, and Edith is about as long-suffering as they come, is willing to do day and night cover. I'm wrapped up in some pretty important deals over the next fortnight and my proposal was for you to work for me between five and ten every evening, Monday to Friday.'

'I'm sorry but that's out of the question.'

'Why?'

'I don't have to give long explanations,' Sunny told him stiffly. Something about the prospect of being inside his house sent shivers through her. No matter that she now knew that he had no interest in her aside from babysitter for his daughter. 'But, in case it's missed you, I actually already have a job after work and it's a job I enjoy and wouldn't want to lose. Also...'

Stefano tilted his head to one side. Flora had been animated on the drive back to the house. In fact, she had been the most animated he'd seen her since she had arrived in London. She had actually spoken to him, as opposed to sitting in surly silence and answering his questions in monosyllables.

'Also...?' he prompted softly.

Sunny shrugged and reddened. 'Nothing. I... I just can't do it. I'm sorry.'

'But you don't know what the terms and conditions are,' he murmured. He wondered what else she had been about to say. She was guarded and that was something he never saw in the women he met. And the way she had rushed into the assumption that he'd been after her for sex. Was she accustomed to having to fend off men? Had she suffered from office pests? They were out there, no question of it, and she had the looks to pro- voke over-enthusiasm in most red-blooded men, he would have thought.

Or maybe one pest in particular had made her suspicious of all men...

He was a little unnerved at the amount of time he was wasting in pointless speculation.

'Unless, of course, you have a boyfriend... someone who might not want you to spend time away from the flat when you're not at work...'

Sunny laughed shortly. 'I wouldn't let any guy tell me what I could or couldn't do.' The words were out before she could take them back. 'By which,' she continued lamely, 'I mean that I'm... my own person...not that it's any business of yours whether I have a boyfriend or not any- way...I just...I'm sorry...'

'I'm sure the restaurant could spare you for a couple of weeks. In fact, I don't see that as a problem at all. I'll personally arrange for a re- placement and cover the costs myself. And with regard to what you earn there...' He paused, al- lowing speculation to take root in her head and spout tendrils. 'I'll quadruple it.' He sat back and watched her narrowly. 'I'd like you to work for me and I'm prepared to pay you far, far more than you would earn in the restaurant, including tips...'

'I don't understand,' Sunny stammered, thoroughly taken aback. 'Why can't you just go and employ someone from an agency?'

'Flora averages a nanny a fortnight and, during that fortnight, I'm bombarded with complaints from whatever nanny happens to be working for me. I don't need that. She's taken a liking to you and I'm prepared to take a gamble.'

'I have no experience of looking after children, Mr Gunn.'

'For God's sake, there's no need to keep calling me Mr Gunn.' He paused and watched her, trying to read behind the cautious exterior.

Agitated, Sunny looked away. 'Don't you have a...um...a partner?'

'Partner?'

'A girlfriend? Someone who could step in and help out?' She had no idea from whence the rumour had sprung that he was interested in Katherine. Maybe the rumours had been wrong. Maybe there was someone else in the background, although it beggared belief that he would bring

work to a new, small company and not use one
of the top guns to handle his business.

'Now, now, Sunny—or shall I call you Miss
Porter as you seem determined to stick to the
formalities?—would you say that you're enti-
tled to ask that question considering you've surrounded yourself with No Trespassing signs?' He
watched her squirm for a few seconds. 'There's
no handy woman ready to jump in and help out.'
He thought of Katherine and his mother's fine
intentions to set him up. Nice enough woman
but he certainly couldn't picture her in the role
of surrogate mother. Indeed, she had seemed dis-
tinctly uncomfortable when presented with Flora.

'What about Flora's mother?' It seemed an
obvious enough question and she was surprised
when the shutters snapped down, coldly locking
her out. As No Trespassing signs went, she'd just
stumbled into an almighty giant-sized one.

'Flora's mother died several months ago,' Stefano said abruptly. 'Now, are you willing to take
the job or not? I've given you my offer and, from
the looks of it, you could do with the money. You
can bring your work to the house if you want to
do overtime and that's an added bonus, considering working in a restaurant doesn't afford that

luxury. And I may be misreading the situation, but if you're intent on a career then the lack of overtime must be a decided drawback to someone young and ambitious.'

'I'm not sure whether it would be entirely ethical for me to work with a client.'

'In which case, I'll take my considerably well-paid work away from your law firm. How does that sound?'

'You wouldn't.' Sunny was aghast at that threat because, if he did that, then the worst-case scenarios would be a great deal worse than the ones she had conjured up in her head when he'd told her that he'd spoken to Katherine.

'Yes. I would. You would be surprised at the lengths I would go to in order to get what I want.' He thought of that small but perceptible change in his daughter on the drive back to his house. For that reason alone it was worth the hassle of being here. He could hardly believe that she was kicking up a fuss at being paid handsomely to do a babysitting job of limited duration. 'And, just for your information, I have already cleared the way with Katherine. I explained the situation and she's more than happy for you to help out.'

'Is she? Didn't she…ah…volunteer to do it herself?'

'Why would she do that?'

'No reason.' Annoyed with herself for being drawn into that faux pas, she stared down at her trainers. 'What if it doesn't work out?'

'I prefer positive thinking. Like I said, Flora doesn't warm to people easily but she warmed to you. It's good enough for me. Now, the job. Yes or no? You'll start first thing on Monday. I'll have my driver collect you from work and return you to your flat. Meals will be provided and you're free to do as you wish with Flora, although she's accustomed to being in bed by eight. I'll open an account for you if you want to take her anywhere. Feel free to use it.'

It was a fantastic opportunity to add to her savings. She knew that. She might even treat herself to some new work clothes. So why was she still hesitating? It was crazy.

'Okay,' she agreed. 'I'll do it. I'll take the job.'

CHAPTER THREE

STEFANO'S HOUSE, on the outskirts of London, was a dream house.

For one man and a young child, it was ridiculously big. There were six bedrooms, five bathrooms, too many undefined reception rooms to count and a kitchen that was spacious enough for a table at one end that could seat ten. It opened out to a spread of perfectly manicured lawns, in the middle of which was a magnificent swimming pool.

Paradise for an eight-year-old child and Sunny wondered whether the pool was used during the day. The weather had certainly been hot enough for swimming.

Life here couldn't have been more different for Flora than her own life had been for her. She wondered what it would have been like had she, as a kid, been exposed to this level of opulence. She would have been terrified.

Now, as an adult, she could see the many material advantages but she was also beginning to see the many drawbacks. After four days of babysitting, she was slowly realising certain things and there was no need for Flora to verbalise them.

Surrounded by all this luxury, Flora was confused and unhappy. Her mother had died and she had been yanked across the ocean to a life she had never known and a father she seemed to resent.

'I hate it here,' she had confided the evening before, as Sunny had been about to switch off the bedroom light and leave the room. 'I want to go back to New Zealand.'

'I get that.' Sunny had sat on the bed. There were no signposts as to how she should connect with a kid and it wasn't in her to be patronising. She had had to grow up fast and that had implanted in her the belief that kids could deal with honesty far better than most adults thought.

They didn't like being patronised and Sunny didn't see why she should patronise Flora.

'Sometimes circumstances change and, when that happens, you just have to go with it because you can never change things back to the way they were. That's just the truth.'

Flora, she had discovered, was as mature as

she herself had been at that age, although not for similar reasons. She was just a grown-up child with shaped opinions and the sort of suspicious, cautious nature that Sunny could understand because she, too, shared those traits. She had no time for her father and Sunny could have told her another harsh truth, which was that she was here and having him around was also something she couldn't change so she might as well accept it.

It wasn't in her brief to broker a relationship between father and daughter, however. In fact, it wasn't in her brief to be curious about the dynamics of the household at all. She was there to babysit, no more, no less, but she liked the kid and she knew that Flora liked her, even though she still didn't understand why because they never did anything Sunny imagined an eight-year-old would find fun. When she'd been eight, there had been no exciting trips to Adventure Parks or shiny new toys. She had taken refuge in books and so pointing Flora in the direction of more serious pursuits came as the natural choice.

They watched telly, always the National Geographic channel which they both enjoyed. They'd played a game of Scrabble and Sunny had laughed and told Flora that she could allow her to win or they could both play to the best of their ability and see what happened. The evening before, after they had eaten an early dinner at six, they had both attempted to bake and it had been a miserable failure.

'I didn't do much baking as a child,' Sunny had said truthfully, 'and I don't think I ever got the hang of it. We'll have to bin the bread. Or else hang onto it in case we need a lethal weapon.' Which had made Flora laugh until she cried.

Between eight and ten Sunny worked and then Stefano would return with his driver.

His presence filled the house. He would stride in and Sunny would know that she'd been bracing herself for the brief encounter. They would exchange a couple of sentences and then the driver would whisk her away back to her flat and once there she would think about him. She tried to fight those thoughts and when she couldn't she uneasily told herself that it was only natural that he was in her head because she was now working for him. If she hadn't been, she would have forgotten all about him, however startling the impact he had made on her had been.

Now, with Flora in bed, Sunny settled down for her two hours' work, which was absolute bliss because it was a luxury she could never had afforded when she'd been working at the restaurant. She was given the most basic of tasks but they tended to be time-consuming and it was good to be able to work her way through them in the peace and quiet of the sprawling mansion.

Having explored all of the rooms on the ground floor, she had settled on the smallest and the cosiest as her work room. It overlooked the back gardens and she enjoyed glancing up and letting her eyes wander over a vista of mown grass, sweeping trees and, in the distance, the open fields onto which the house backed. Compared to the view from the flat she shared, which gave onto the grimy pavements outside and a lone tree which looked as though it was pining to be anywhere but on a road in London, the view here was breathtaking and it made her feel as though she was on holiday.

Legs tucked under her, her long hair untidily pulled over one shoulder, she was hardly aware of Stefano's appearance in the doorway until he spoke and then she yelped in shock, eyes adjusting to the impressive sight of him.

When she could predict his arrival back, she had time to brace herself for the physical impact he still seemed to have on her. With no time to prepare herself, she could only stare while her heart sped up and her mouth went dry.

He was tugging his tie off, dragging it down so that he could undo the top two buttons of his white shirt, and she tried her best not to gape at the sliver of brown skin exposed.

'What are you doing here?' she stammered, gathering the bits of paper spread around her and smartly shutting her computer.

'I live here.'

'Yes, but...'

'No need to rush, Sunny. I'm back early so we can have a catch-up.'

'A catch-up? On what?'

Stefano banked down a flare of irritation. Her desperation not to be in his company had not abated. They crossed paths when he returned from work and she was always packed up, jacket on, exchanging a few sentences on the move as she headed out the front door. Whatever she did with Flora, she was doing it right because his daughter, when prompted, actually now deigned to show some interest in his questions rather than sullenly sitting at the breakfast table in front of her cellphone playing games. The top-of-the-range cellphone, in retrospect, had not been the cleverest purchase on the planet.

'I haven't eaten,' he said evenly, keen eyes noting the blonde length of her hair which, for once, wasn't tied back, probably an omission because she hadn't expected him home at eight-thirty. 'Why don't you join me in the kitchen?'

'Of course,' Sunny dutifully replied. She sneaked a covert look as he rolled up his shirt-sleeves, exposing muscled forearms sprinkled with dark hair. Everything about him was intensely masculine and her body behaved in disconcerting ways when she was confronted with it.

He was already moving off towards the kitchen and she followed, taking all her work with her and her bag so that she could leg it at speed as soon as their catch-up was finished.

'Drink?' He moved to the wine cooler, which was built into the range of pale cupboards, and extracted a bottle of white wine.

'No, thank you.'

'Relax, Sunny. One drink isn't going to hurt you.' Without giving her time for a second polite refusal, he poured them both a glass, handed one

to her and rummaged for ingredients for a sandwich. 'How are you finding the job?'

'Fine,' she said awkwardly and he turned round
and looked at her with a frown.

'Is that going to be the full extent of your con-
tribution to this conversation?' he asked coolly.
'Monosyllabic answers? Flora talks about you.'

'Does she?' She fiddled with her hair and reminded herself that this was a perfectly normal
business conversation, that of course he would
be interested in knowing what she did with his
daughter. But she still felt horribly nervous and
she knew it was because she was too *aware* of
him for her own good. If this strange reaction
was her body reminding her that she was still
alive, then she resented the reminder.

'Tell me what you two do together.' He dragged
out a chair, sat down and began tucking into his
sandwich.

'Oh, the usual.' Their eyes met and she reddened. Did she really want him asking why she
was so jumpy around him? No. But he would
if she continued to stutter and stammer and, as
he had pointed out, answer his questions with
unhelpful monosyllables. 'Nothing very child-

oriented, I'm afraid, although we did do a spot of baking yesterday after dinner.'

'A failure, I've been told.'

'I'm not very good when it comes to stuff like that,' she said vaguely.

'No mother-daughter bonding sessions in front of a stove?'

'No.' Sunny heard the tightness creep into her voice and she lowered her eyes. 'Nothing like that.'

A girl with secrets. Was he really interested in finding out what those secrets were? Did he care one way or another? She was here to do a job and she was doing a damn fine job. Then she'd be gone…

He found his curiosity unsettling because it was something he never felt with any of the women he dated. He had been through one disastrous relationship and now he made sure to keep everything light and superficial when it came to the opposite sex. Curiosity was definitely neither light nor superficial.

But it was something she roused in him for no reason he could begin to understand.

'I think Flora's unhappy and lonely.' She rushed into saying more than she had intended because she didn't want him quizzing her about her past. Being here had brought home to her the differences in their worlds and she didn't want him judging her because of her background. She was an aspiring lawyer, coerced into doing an impromptu job for him. She didn't want him feeling sorry for her or pitying her.

'I mean…she's been displaced from everything she knew and I just get the feeling that she hasn't settled here just yet. She hasn't mentioned her school once and that's saying something.'

Stefano shoved his plate to one side and sat back, arms folded behind his head. 'Is that right?' he drawled and Sunny bristled.

'She's just a child and she's had to endure some pretty major life changes.' The way he was staring at her with those dark, dark speculative eyes made her feel all hot and bothered and she was suddenly as angry with him as she was with herself for feeling so *exposed*.

'And I hope you don't mind me being honest,' she said tersely, 'but I don't suppose it helps that you work such long hours.' *Oh, he's never here*, Flora had shrugged apropos of nothing in particular a couple of evenings ago, and Sunny had heard the hurt in her voice and been moved by it.

Stefano stiffened at the implied criticism in her voice, yet she was only stating the obvious, wasn't she? He wondered when positive criticism had become something he could do without. He certainly never encountered it in his day-to-day life.

'It's impossible for me to conduct a nine-to-five existence.'

Sunny shrugged. 'It's none of my business anyway.'

Perversely, the fact that she was happy to back away from the contentious conversation rather than pursue it made him want to prolong it. 'Don't start conversations you don't want to finish,' he inserted. 'I'm a big boy. I can take whatever you have to say to me. Did Flora tell you that?'

'A passing remark. Look—' Sunny raised her eyes to his and felt heat creep into her face '—I'm not here to have opinions on…on…how you handle Flora. I'm just here in a babysitting capacity. I need the money. I don't suppose any of your nannies tell you what they really think because they'd just be here to do a babysitting job, like me.'

'They don't tell me what they think because they're intimidated by me,' Stefano said drily.

'You don't like being around me but you're not intimidated by me. At least, that's the impression I've got. Am I wrong?'

Sunny had no idea how they had got where they had but this felt like a very personal conversation. Or maybe it was the intimacy of being in the kitchen with him, just the two of them, that made it feel more personal than it really was.

'Well?' he prompted. 'True or false?'

'I try not to be intimidated by anyone,' she was spurred into responding.

'And that works for you?'

'Yes. Yes, it does.' Colour flared in her cheeks but she held his gaze defiantly. 'I like to think, *What's the worst that can happen?* I mean, you can sack me from this job but, if you do, then that's fine. I'd be more than happy to return to my restaurant work.'

'Long hours,' he mused, startling her by the sudden change of topic.

'What do you mean?'

'When do you get time to relax? Do you have a busy social life on the weekends?'

'I'm too busy building a career to have a busy social life on the weekends,' she snapped.

'How old are you?'

'I'm twenty-four, although I don't see what my age has to do with anything.'

'Katherine told me that you're one of the most dedicated employees in the company. You're in by eight every morning, sometimes earlier, and if you leave promptly for your job in the restaurant it never seems to affect the quality of your work, which is always of the highest standard. Which means, I'm guessing, that you work on weekends…'

Sunny was torn between pleasure that her hard work had been noted and dismay that she had been a topic of discussion. 'You have to work hard in order to get on,' she muttered, flushing.

'To the extent that it consumes your every waking hour?'

'It seems that work consumes all *your* waking hours,' Sunny said defensively. 'I'm sorry. I shouldn't have said that, Mr Gunn.'

'If you call me Mr Gunn again, I'll sack you.'

She didn't know whether he was joking or not and she bit back the temptation to keep arguing with him.

'And, believe it or not, work doesn't consume *all* my waking hours,' he told her softly, 'I know how to play as well…'

Sunny stared. The tenor of his voice was so…
sexy…and when she looked at him it felt as
though his eyes were boring straight past her de-
fences, seeing into parts of her that were soft and
yielding and vulnerable, parts of her that hadn't
been forced into toughening up over the years.

'I…I…' Her voice was cracked and she cleared
her throat. 'I plan on getting through my LPC
exams and then…then I'll have plenty of time to
go out and have fun…more than enough time…'
Because, right now, clubbing and going to pubs
and bars just wasn't on the agenda.

When did she ever have fun?

That was something that she never really
thought about. A history of insecurity and root-
lessness had instilled in her a need to ground herself, to have the security she had missed out on
and that security, she had always known, would
come in the form of her career. She had learned
to distrust the attention she got from men and she
had learned that at an early age, so fun, for her,
wasn't about guys and dates and flirting. Her one
stab at *fun* had run aground and she wasn't going
to repeat the experience. She just didn't have it in
her to enjoy life the way other girls her age did.

As she'd told her young charge, what you couldn't change you simply had to accept, like it or not.

So fun for her wasn't about all those things girls her age were interested in.

Suddenly the life she was looking at, the life she had strived with every ounce of her being to secure, looked empty and lacking.

Stefano watched the play of expression on her face. There was a luminosity to her face and a guilelessness that was at odds with the tough exterior.

His eyes drifted lower, to the jut of her breasts underneath the T-shirt. Small breasts, a neat handful. He drew his breath in sharply at the unexpected image of her in his king-sized bed, with all that blonde hair across his pillow…lying naked and hot for him.

His erection was as swift as it was hard and painful, bulging against the zip, and now that his imagination had taken flight, it was flying without restraint.

What would it feel like to have her delicate tongue flicking against his shaft? How would she taste? He imagined her writhing under his exploring mouth and hands, twisting and moaning and begging, desperate for him to take her.

She was too young to be so utterly controlled and he wanted to smash through that control and see what was underneath...

Hell, where were his thoughts going? Aside from anything else, there was no way he was going to jeopardise the tenuous, fragile shoots of a relationship tentatively trying to establish themselves with Flora by hitting on her babysitter.

He shifted uncomfortably, trying to ease the pain of his erection, annoyed with himself for his utter lack of self-control. 'There's another reason I wanted to talk to you.' He dragged his brain back into gear but for a few seconds he had to look outside rather than at her face. 'I have to be at a breakfast meeting on Saturday and I want to ask you whether you would step in and cover here. Naturally, you will be paid handsomely for putting yourself out...'

'Saturday...'

'Day after tomorrow.'

Her fingers were slender and she was raking them through her tangle of fine hair now, frowning slightly as though he had posed a particularly tricky maths problem which she had been called upon to solve rather than being asked a simple question that required a simple yes or no answer.

'You can bring your work,' he reminded her, 'although you might want to do something…a little more fun…unless you have plans for the weekend? Have you?'

More than anything Sunny would have loved to have told him that she had. In fact, she had planned on getting ahead with some studying and then having a lazy night in because Amy was going to be out on another date with yet another hopeless boyfriend.

'What about the woman who stays with Flora during the daytime?' she asked and Stefano shook his head.

He laughed shortly. 'She's been with Flora for a fortnight and so far she hasn't run screaming for the hills. I don't want to test her patience by asking her for anything beyond the call of duty.'

Sunny felt her lips twitch in a smile. It was bad enough that he was so distractingly attractive. Add a wry sense of humour into the mix and that attraction became combustible.

'Why have you run through so many nannies?' She was genuinely perplexed because Flora seemed a far from difficult child.

'She hasn't wanted to have a nanny so she's made sure to get rid of them,' Stefano said shortly. He stood up and poured them both another glass of wine. 'I mistakenly assumed that someone young and enthusiastic would be the first choice but they've all found her stubborn refusal to communicate unbearably frustrating...'

'I don't try and force her into having fun,' Sunny mused thoughtfully.

'Edith, the woman who comes in during the day to help out, is sixty-three years old, although she's already mentioned that she doesn't like the way Flora talks to her.'

'Which is how?'

'Patronisingly.'

Sunny wondered whether Flora's patronising wasn't a response to the older woman also being patronising and then was surprised that she was finding excuses for her young charge and taking her side over a woman she hadn't even met.

'I... Okay, that's fine.' She stood up and felt the two glasses of wine rush to her head. 'What time would you like me to come on Saturday?'

'My driver will collect you at ten and I'll need you for the whole day, I'm afraid. I won't be home until at least nine in the evening.'

Stefano thought that she looked like someone who had suddenly remembered that she should be fleeing the scene of the crime instead of hanging around making small talk with the officer in charge.

'And don't forget that you have full use of the account. You have the card. Take advantage of it.'

They were at the front door. When Sunny looked up, she felt her heart skip a beat because he was so close to her, almost but not quite invading her space.

For a second, a brief destabilising second, instead of wanting to step back, she wanted to move closer, wanted to place the palm of her hand on his chest and feel the hardness of muscle under her fingers.

'Perhaps I will,' she said shortly, swerving away and opening the door. 'And there's no need for Eric to drive me home.' She felt breathless, as though she'd been running a marathon and now had to steady herself or else fall over from the exertion. 'I can make my way to the station. It's only a half hour walk and the exercise will do me good.'

'I wouldn't hear of it,' Stefano murmured, not taking his eyes from her face even though he was already on his cellphone calling his driver to the front.

Sunny felt herself break out in a fine film of perspiration and she stuck her hands behind her back, clasping her computer case between them and clutching it for dear life.

This was what it felt like to be *turned on* and it was the first time it had ever happened to her. John had never *turned her on*. She had liked him, perhaps even loved him in the way you loved a dear, dear friend, but this overwhelming physical helplessness had been absent.

She didn't know why it had chosen to make an appearance now but she knew that it was utterly inappropriate and complete madness and was to be stamped out at all costs.

Sunny had no idea what she was going to do with Flora on Saturday but the day dawned with the promise of heat.

She had grown up in London and now lived in London and so escaping London, going to Stefano's sprawling mansion in Berkshire always felt like a sneaky escape and even more so now because it was the weekend.

On the spur of the moment, she packed a little bag and thought that if it was hot enough she might dip her feet in the pool.

She'd asked Flora whether she swam in it at all and was told that of course she did.

'I learned to swim when I was two,' she had told Sunny proudly. 'We had a swimming pool in our house in New Zealand and Annie used to take me twice a week to the public pool so that I could get practice swimming with other girls. In competitions. I always won.'

'I bet your mother was proud of you,' Sunny had said, because *she* would have been proud, but her mother, she was informed, had rarely gone to stuff like that because it was boring.

'She liked going out,' Flora had said, shrugging her shoulders, 'parties and stuff. She liked dressing up.'

Lonely on both sides of the world, Sunny had thought. You could be lonely even if you had loads of money because loneliness was very fair and even-handed when it decided to pay a visit. No distinctions were ever made.

Eric came to collect her promptly at ten, always on time, and she allowed herself a sigh of pure anticipation at spending the day out, doing something other than working or household chores. Plus Amy was overjoyed to have the flat to herself for the day.

'I'm going to show him that I can be a domestic goddess,' she had confided.

'Brilliant idea.'

'Something Thai,' Amy had said vaguely. 'A salad or something. Don't worry. I'll be gone by the time you get home...'

Sunny had wondered whether some sort of Thai salad was going to work with her friend's latest big love interest but who was she to say anything? She had images in her head of a guy who was inappropriate on so many levels that it made her feel dizzy when she thought about it.

But today she would just relax and enjoy herself because she had one more week and then she'd be gone.

She'd miss Flora.

In her own way, Flora was as fragile as she had been at that age and Sunny felt a pang when she thought about saying goodbye and walking away, leaving her in the capable hands of another nanny.

It was already baking hot by the time the driver pulled into the long drive that led up to the house. She expected to find Stefano there, had braced herself for some polite conversation but she was greeted at the door by the housekeeper, who came, it would seem, to clean on the weekends.

'We could do something exciting and fun,' she suggested to Flora, racking her brain to think of what might fit the bill. 'Perhaps a zoo...or a park...maybe the movies...or something...'

'I disapprove of zoos,' Flora ruled out that option immediately and Sunny grinned.

'Or we could just...have lunch somewhere nice and then come back here...'

'And swim!'

'I'll have to stay in the shallow end...'

'Why?'

'Because I...I never actually learned how to swim...'

'I'll teach you!'

With a project in hand, Flora was happy to rush through the various *fun* things Sunny felt she should be doing. The zoo, which would have meant trekking back into London, was fortunately ruled out and instead they went to a nearby beauty spot for a picnic. There was a huge lake, acres of woodland and many, many people also out enjoying the area with their kids and their dogs.

Flora talked about New Zealand, about what

she had done there and about the open spaces and natural beauty. Her mother rarely featured in these accounts, except in passing, and her father not at all. Had he been over to see her at all? Sunny wondered. Or had he washed his hands of his own child the second he had obtained a divorce? Strangely, although he was a workaholic and although, as far as Sunny was concerned, he needed to take way more interest in his daughter, she didn't see him as the sort of guy who would ever walk away from responsibility.

Walking around the lake, she realised that speculating about Stefano Gunn was becoming a full-time occupation. When she wasn't thinking about work she was thinking about him and having told herself that there was no way she would allow herself to be curious about him or his circumstances, she still was.

Eric, fortunately, was there to save them the huge walk back in blistering sunshine and it was a little after two by the time Sunny had stripped down to the modest black bikini she had brought with her.

She had always wanted to know how to swim. Indeed, she had started a few swimming lessons less than a year ago but time had been in short supply and she had stopped them. The fact was that her life had just been too disordered, too unpredictable for something as constant as swimming lessons and when she had earned her scholarship to the boarding school she had made sure to steer clear of the enormous swimming pool. With few close friends, no one had questioned her reluctance to go swimming and, as it was a voluntary after-school activity, there had been no awkward or embarrassing confessions about her lack of know-how.

But this glittering turquoise pool in the calm peace of the countryside was irresistible.

She stayed at the shallow end and watched a different Flora prance around, diving and flipping and swimming underwater like a little darting fish.

Instructions were given, with Flora stepping into the role of stern swimming teacher.

Little by little, Sunny relaxed and began enjoying the weightless feeling of being in the water. It was a very big pool and she tentatively edged away from the shallow end, growing in confidence as she remembered some of the instructions from her brief foray into swimming lessons months before.

Don't panic and swallow lungfuls of water while trying to scrabble and touch ground...

Brilliant, sensible advice.

Except...

How was she to know that Stefano wouldn't do as he had promised? Wouldn't stay out of the house until at least nine in the evening? In other words, how could she have guessed that, daringly halfway across the pool, trying her luck with paddling from one side to the other, she would look up and see him? Standing right there? Looking right back down at her?

All the brilliant, sensible advice flew straight out of her head. She panicked. She gulped down water and panicked more, scrabbling to touch ground but, in her confusion, sinking and flailing.

Flora was the first to dive in, slicing through the water and grasping her under her arms.

Convinced that she was on the verge of drowning, Sunny still wanted to yell to her that she was way too young to be trying a rescue mission on an adult.

But she didn't have to because Stefano wasn't far behind his daughter and then bigger, stronger arms were around her, firmly gripping her ribcage and pulling her with consummate ease to the side of the pool, where he heaved her out with no trouble at all.

'Good job, Flora,' she heard him say, to which Flora muttered something in reply, but when Sunny opened her eyes and looked at her she was blushing as she turned away for a towel, which she brought to her.

Humiliation washed over her in waves. She could barely look at him and, when she did, he was leaning over her with a concerned expression.

He was soaking wet. He'd kicked his shoes off before diving into the pool but he was dripping.

Sunny squeezed her eyes tightly shut and prayed that she had somehow imagined the whole horrible episode but when she opened them he was even closer to her, kneeling with his big hand propping up her head.

The spluttering was thankfully done but shock was setting in.

'We need to get you upstairs.' He'd taken the

towel from Flora and sat her up so that he could wrap the towel around her as best he could.

'No,' Sunny pleaded. 'I'm fine.' She was trembling violently even though she was doing her best not to.

'Flora—' he turned to his daughter '—do you want to start running a bath for Sunny? And make sure there's a dry towel there. And Flora… you would make a fine lifeguard, once you've grown a little…' He smiled crookedly and felt a burst of something he had never felt before— sheer pleasure and warmth when she half smiled back at him. 'Change into some dry clothes before you run the bath,' he instructed. 'And then wait for us in the sitting room. We need to do something a little special after this…'

'Okay. 'Cos she'll probably be all shaken up.'

'Exactly.' He turned back to Sunny as Flora disappeared inside the house. 'And you,' he murmured, 'I don't want to hear a peep out of you… you've had a shock. Just relax and let your breathing return to normal.'

Relax?

When her practically naked body was pressed against him? When his arms were so close to her breasts that one inadvertent shift in position could have him touching her? When her head was against his chest and she could almost hear the beating of his heart under his wet suit?

After this, there was no way she could stay on here…

CHAPTER FOUR

SUNNY HAD NOT explored this section of the house. She knew where Flora's room was because she settled her to bed but all the other rooms were always closed off and somehow it would have felt nosy to open doors and peer inside.

So she had no idea where she was being taken and she was far too busy trying to deal with her mortification to give that much thought.

She heard the sound of a bath being run and when she opened her eyes she could instantly see that she was in Stefano's room. It was massive, with a super-king-sized bed in solid dark wood dominating one side of the wall. Everything in the room was overwhelmingly *male*, from the dark wood of the bed and the chest of drawers, to the sleek lines of the built-in wardrobes and the lush fall of deep burgundy velvet curtains that had been pulled back to offer spectacular views of the rolling lawns at the back.

Including, she suspected, the treacherous swimming pool, which had glittered so temptingly before subjecting her to this horrendous attack of pure humiliation.

He kicked the door to the en-suite bathroom fully open and deposited her gently on the chair by the window.

Immediately, he began undoing the buttons of his shirt and Sunny nearly leaped out of the chair in horrified consternation.

'What are you doing?' she yelped and he shot her a dry look.

'I'm getting out of my wet clothes to forestall an attack of pneumonia. Where are your dry clothes?'

'I changed in the bathroom downstairs. They're…they're in my backpack. Please, there's no need for all of this.'

He didn't answer. Instead, he continued getting out of his clothes as he vanished out of the bathroom and she distantly heard him shouting to Flora to hunt down the backpack and bring it up. When he reappeared, he had changed and the bath was now completely run. Lots of bubbles. Sunny could barely bring herself to look at it.

'You're probably in a state of mild shock.' He tested the water with one hand and just then

Flora appeared with the backpack and hovered by the door.

'I was teaching Sunny how to swim,' she offered.

Stefano shot her a frowning, questioning look. 'She doesn't know how to swim? You're eight and you swim like a champion… We're going to have to have a race one of these days. I can't believe…'

'I know. It's silly.'

'It *is* a little odd.'

'Would you two mind not discussing me as though I'm not here?' Sunny was burning up with embarrassment and even more so when Flora looked at her with an eight-year-old's sympathy.

'You were doing really well until…'

'Yes…well…' There was no way she was going to get into any conversation about how Stefano's sudden appearance at the side of the pool had thrown her into a tailspin. 'If the two of you wouldn't mind, I'll have this bath now…' Not, she wanted to add, that she needed one.

But the bikini, drying on her, was cloying and uncomfortable and she felt horribly exposed in it, her nipples tight from the damp cold, pushing like bullets against the fine, stretchy fabric.

When she glanced down she could see her own shadowy cleavage and her bare stomach and her legs.

She wanted to burst into tears but, instead, she stared down at the pale tiled floor and almost collapsed with relief when they both left the bathroom, quietly shutting the door behind them, a door which she made sure to lock.

She sank into the bath, which was blissful because she had been colder than she had thought, and she closed her eyes, letting the warm water wash over her.

What was happening to her? It had been a shock for her to discover, having written off her sexuality, that she could find a man so blindingly attractive. But this wasn't just any man and she knew that even if she might react to those incidental touches, that sort of reaction was purely on her side.

Stefano Gunn was out of her league. Over the past two years, after she and John had broken up, many men had looked at her, made passes at her, some crude, others more subtle, but she had never been interested. None of them had penetrated the hard outer shell she had taken pains to develop around herself and she still couldn't understand how it was that Stefano, without even trying, had managed to do so.

She had always considered herself immune to the superficial tug of lust. She had learned lessons from her flawed parent and then, later, having to always be on guard against the covert, greedy glances of her foster father, she had developed an edge of cynicism that had never left her.

Even the more open, healthy appreciation from the boys she had met when she had been at the boarding school and after, at university, had failed to get past her inherent wariness and when the one man she'd felt she should have been able to really open up to had failed to excite her in that way, she had firmly shut the door on physical attraction.

Stefano didn't look at her at all and yet...flustered her. When he did look at her, it was as if she was plugged into an electric socket and there was no part of her body that didn't respond.

Was it because he was so out of her league? Because there was no danger of him taking any interest in her?

Was it the sort of silly schoolgirl crush that made teenagers stick posters of pop stars on their bedroom walls? Was that it? Something passing, harmless and hardly surprising?

She uneasily told herself that that was exactly what it was because she knew that when and if she ever tested the waters again, ever felt inclined to go on a date, then it would be with someone safe, someone who wouldn't make her feel vulnerable and out of control. True, John had filled that specification but because that particular relationship hadn't worked out didn't mean that the parameters for all future relationships should change. They shouldn't. Logic decreed that.

And when had she ever not listened to the unwavering voice of logic?

Listening to her head, paying calm heed to what it told her when her own young life had been in such disarray through no fault of her own, had always worked.

Feeling a bit better, she opened the door and there he was, lying on the bed in a pair of faded jeans and an old T-shirt with his computer on his stomach. He snapped it shut and eased himself off the bed.

'I was beginning to think about breaking the door down to make sure you hadn't drowned in the bath…'

Caught on the back foot, Sunny could only stare. He looked so effortlessly elegant. The low-slung jeans did amazing things for his physique and the T-shirt clung in a way that showed off the muscled strength of his arms. And he was barefoot. She hurriedly looked away.

'I'm sorry about that,' Sunny said stiffly. She eyed the open door and headed towards it. 'Perhaps—' she cleared her throat '—I might have a quick word with you.'

'I'm surprised you haven't asked me why I'm back so early. Did you start floundering because you weren't expecting to see me?'

'I...' They began trotting down the stairs, she quickly, he taking his time but still keeping pace.

'Because I wouldn't like you being so nervous in my presence that it becomes life-threatening.'

Sunny rounded on him, arms folded. 'Are you laughing at me?'

'How is it that you've never had swimming lessons?'

'I...I...' She went red and looked away. 'Where's Flora?'

'Happily ensconced in front of the television in the sitting room. I told her you would probably need a little time to gather yourself after your skirmish in the pool. I thought that swimming lessons were compulsory for all school-children...'

'They probably are!'

'Did you have an early aversion to water?'

Sunny glared. 'I would have loved to have had swimming lessons,' she gritted. 'But that never happened to me.' She spun on her heel, heart beating wildly inside her and made for the kitchen. She would have to hand in her notice. How could she not? What sort of babysitter ended up having to be rescued from a dangerous situation by the young child she was in charge of babysitting? He would never trust her around his daughter again.

And maybe that was for the best, she thought. He did weird things to her, things she didn't like, and if he wasn't around then life would get back to normal without that jumpy, sickening feeling inside her that she'd been carrying around for days.

And maybe, she further thought, she could address some of his curiosity about her. Curiosity about why she spent all her time working, why she needed money so badly, why she'd never learned how to swim...

Maybe it would be a good thing for those glaring differences between them to be brought out into the open. The way she'd been brought up was something that had been out of her control but maybe vocalising it would be a timely reminder to her of the idiocy of harbouring delusional fantasies about him. It would also kill off his curiosity stone-dead because he certainly wouldn't keep prying for extraneous information when he knew that he might be provided with information that would make him feel uncomfortable. Rich people always, but always, felt uncomfortable when they were treated to tales of hardship, poverty or despair.

But mostly, if her body kept ignoring the fact that he was from a different world, then wasn't it time that her head took control?

'I just want to say...' She turned to him the minute they were in the kitchen, making sure to keep her voice low just in case Flora decided that the television programme she was watching wasn't as much fun as seeking out her nearly drowned babysitter, to whom she'd been giving swimming lessons. 'I just want to say,' she repeated, 'that I'm handing in my resignation.' She tried a laugh. 'It goes down as the shortest job in history.'

'What are you talking about? Why are you handing in your resignation?' She'd washed her hair but already the late-afternoon heat was drying it, throwing blonde strands in stark relief. It hung down her back, almost to her waist. And she didn't wear make-up. He had never known a woman who didn't lather on the war-paint the second she was out of the bath. But her skin was satiny-smooth and clear. His gaze lingered on her ripe, full lips and he looked away because he could already feel his body stirring into life. Once again. Just as it had when he'd been holding her, wet and trembling, against him and as light as a feather despite the fact that she was tall.

He'd had a battle not to stare at the plump thrust of her breasts under the bikini top, not to get trapped by the sight of that tightened nipple poking against the wet cloth. She had been utterly unaware of just how revealing the swimsuit was and, thankfully, just as utterly unaware of the effect it had been having on him.

It seemed his body had decided to raise two fingers to common sense. He'd never had to deal with self-denial and he was finding it difficult.

He wondered whether his mother would have been amused by the fact that the woman she had done her best to set him up with had left him cold while the office junior was sending his blood pressure into the stratosphere.

The difficult, stubborn office junior whom he'd had to cajole into this job. The job she was now talking about ditching.

'Because I think it's safe to say that I failed.' She looked away quickly. 'You didn't pay me to...to...'

'Endanger your life?'

'I should never have gone anywhere near that swimming pool considering I can barely doggy-paddle from one side to the next.'

'You're good for Flora and I wouldn't dream of accepting your resignation.' And that, he reminded himself heavily, was why he couldn't do what he wanted to do. She was good for Flora and, in turn, that was proving to be good for his relationship with his daughter and he wasn't going to risk fooling around with that...

'You don't have to say that,' Sunny said fiercely.

'You're right. I don't. So why don't you just take me at my word?' He ran his fingers through his hair and stood up to pour them both some water.

'You've probably had enough of this stuff for the day. Want something stronger?'

'This is fine. But you don't pay me to get myself in situations where I need rescuing.'

'I haven't rescued a damsel in distress for a while. Maybe it was time that I brushed up on the skill.' He looked at her over the rim of the glass and was surprised at how vulnerable she seemed. Scratch a little under the surface and it was easy to reach the person who didn't spend her every waking moment doing her job and keeping the world at bay.

Was that why he found her so intensely appealing? She made him feel young again for reasons he couldn't quite put his finger on. He was thirty-one and most of the time he felt much older. But something about her...

Was it the same thing that appealed to his daughter?

He fought to stop the senseless speculation.

'I don't need rescuing,' she heard herself say. 'And I've never been a damsel in distress. In fact, I disapprove of all those limp women who think that they need rescuing by some big, strong guy...'

'Is that your way of telling me that you think

I'm big and strong?' He caught her eye, raised his eyebrows and grinned crookedly, unable to help himself. 'So tell me why you've never learned to swim.'

Sunny took a deep breath. Would he be amused if he knew her background? Pity she would find hard to tolerate but she somehow didn't think that he would pity her. Certainly, it would reposition the lines between them which, for him, were clear but for her too blurred for comfort.

She was an underling in a company he could buy ten times over. Had he given them the job because of Katherine? She didn't know. What she did know was that Katherine was far more in his league than she was so it was totally out of order for her to even look at him in any way other than someone way down the pecking order who was working for him.

Get the boundary lines back in place, at least in her mind, and maybe she would stop responding like the teenager she no longer was. And he would keep his distance, too.

'I guess you think that I'm like all the other people who work for the company,' she said, tilting her chin and maintaining eye contact, even though she could read nothing on his face.

'Do I? Tell me what you think I think about all the other people who work for the company. I'm all ears...bearing in mind I haven't met most of them...'

Sunny blushed. Explaining about her past was something she had never done. The other kids at the boarding school into which she had been accepted had known that her circumstances had not been like theirs, had known that she had been given a scholarship, one of only three full scholarships awarded to kids from underprivileged backgrounds.

But she had never talked about hers.

There was no reason to talk about it now but something in her head was telling her that she had to recognise the lines drawn in the sand between them because she couldn't understand her response to him and she was desperate to keep it at bay.

She needed to tell him more for her sake than for his.

And part of her...wanted to.

'I didn't have a cosseted childhood,' she said steadily. 'In fact, I had a pretty awful time growing up, although I just accepted it for what it was and never really spent too much time thinking of how it could have been different. I learned early on that what you can't change you just have to accept...'

She remembered the way Flora had, very briefly, communicated with her father and allowed him into her world and she wondered whether her words of advice had been taken on board. *Accept the things you can't change.*

Stefano was listening intently, his head ever so slightly tilted to one side.

When women launched into anecdotes about their past, they did it to try and engage his attention and encourage his interest.

He didn't get the feeling that she was trying to encourage his interest.

There was an underlying defiance to her voice that made him wonder whether she was even trying to engage his attention at all or whether she was, in some obscure way, trying to warn him off.

Surely not.

Surely she couldn't have noticed the effect she had on him. For once, he was in the company of a woman who was...unpredictable. A woman he couldn't read, a woman who wasn't out to impress him.

Throw sexy into the mix and was it any wonder that she turned him on?

'Tell me,' he encouraged huskily and he caught the wary look she shot him from under her lashes.

'Most of the people I work with come from good, solid, middle-class backgrounds.' She stared at her fingers, inspecting her fingernails while talking. 'I don't have a problem with that. It's great, but a good, solid, middle-class background was so far out of my reach when I was a kid...' She sighed and stopped fidgeting to look him squarely in the eyes. 'My mother drank and took drugs. She was weak, easily influenced by men, and I spent my childhood never knowing what life was going to bring from one day to the next. There were times when I was taken into care and other times when there were little periods of stability. My schooling was patchy and then, when I was still far too young, my mother died from an overdose and I was taken into care permanently. Eventually I was fostered, which was a nightmare, and thankfully I managed to win a scholarship to a prestigious boarding school. In between all of that, there was no opportunity to really crack on with the swimming lessons.' She smiled wryly. 'It was all I could do to make sure I kept ahead with my schoolwork, to be honest.'

'Why did you choose to tell me...?'

'Because you were curious. Hence your question about how it was that I couldn't swim. In your world, there's no such thing as an adult who doesn't know how to swim. I think, in your world, most people don't know what it's like to grow up without their own private swimming pool and holidays abroad by the sea.'

Stefano didn't say anything. She was beginning to make sense to him. He was beginning to understand the layers she had constructed to protect herself and he was also beginning to understand why it was so important for her to work hard and build a career.

A career would be something tangible she could hold onto and he guessed that, after a turbulent childhood, that would mean a lot to her.

And she was right. He'd been curious about her. He'd wanted to find out what made her tick even though it went against his better judgement.

Sunny shrugged. 'I don't share details of my past with people as a rule,' she explained, 'but neither is it some great big secret and it was easier to just fill you in than to have you constantly asking pointed questions. Also, you should know because you might want to change your mind about hiring me as a babysitter for Flora.'

'Why would I change my mind?'

'Because…' Flustered, she looked away.

'Because you think I'm probably a snob…'

'I don't think anything. I was just…giving you the opportunity… Anyway, it doesn't matter. I'm more than happy to continue working for you until the end of next week. Who will be taking over after I've gone? Have you managed to secure another nanny?'

She was a wrong-side-of-the-tracks girl and she had made sure to tell him that, made sure to point out their differences, because she had picked up something. Probably she hadn't even consciously registered it, but she had picked up something, some vibe he had been giving off, and she was firing a warning shot from the bows.

Except when had he become the sort of guy who got scared at warnings being fired? His learning curve at the hands of his ex-wife had freed him from any hesitations when it came to women. He played fair, he laid out the rules of the game and within those constraints it had never, not once, occurred to him, *ever*, that he might allow anything of himself to get out of control. He'd buried his emotions so deep that he had no idea where they were or if he would ever be able to find them and that suited him.

So if she was trying to warn him off by filling him in on the horrors of her background...

She truly must think him a crashing snob.

'My mother usually helps out. Right now, as I have explained, she's in Scotland but she will pick up the slack until I can secure someone else. Flora gets along with my mother slightly better than she gets along with me, which is not terribly well, but at least she isn't outright rude, as she's enjoyed being with the nannies I've hired in the past. Now, why don't I get Eric to drop you at your flat, just long enough for you to change into something a little more dressy? I intend to take you both out for dinner, as I happen to be home much earlier than expected.'

'No! Thank you. I... If you're here, then I should be getting back.' Which would come as a major blow to Amy, who was probably, right now, in full-blown domestic-goddess mode.

'Nonsense,' Stefano said smoothly. 'I insist.' He stood up and dialled his driver, whose lodgings were in a cottage on the grounds. 'I've tried meals out with my daughter,' he admitted with a trace less of his usual self-assurance, 'and the success rate has been zero. When my mother comes, the situation is slightly less fraught but I've noticed small changes in Flora and I can only thank you for that.' He gave his words time to sink in. 'I think,' he continued honestly, 'if you came there might be a marked change of atmosphere.'

Why did the thought of having a meal out with him make her feel so jumpy? Flora would be there! Yet the thought of getting dressed up… turned it from a casual chat into *an occasion.*

But she'd told him about herself, had mentally reinforced the differences between them. Hadn't she killed off all stupid notions of romance? She wasn't tempted by bridal magazines and she didn't peer at engagement rings in the windows of local jewellers. She'd sharpened up her act over the years and, anyway, she'd been born streetwise. She knew that there was a big difference between finding a guy attractive and knowing that he would be rubbish as a long-term investment and she would never allow herself to get wrapped up in anyone who would turn out to be a rubbish long-term investment. Her financial long-term investments were carefully thought out. Her emotional ones would be the same. She'd made that her life's work.

So she was safe as houses when it came to Stefano Gunn, and sparing him no detail about her background—so very, very different from his—was just another safeguard in place.

Just for one bleak moment she stood back and looked at herself. So tough, so sensible, head always screwed on...

It made sense!

It was important to have full control... She'd lived a life where there had been no control; she'd seen how complete lack of control had destroyed her mother...

So here she was, letting her head work through her life options instead of her emotions...

Yet...

For just a few fleeting seconds she was shaken and disconcerted by a sort of raw *envy* of Amy's trusting outlook on the world, her open, hopeful view of men, the enthusiasm with which she flung herself into relationships which Sunny could see would never work.

For a few fleeting seconds she wondered whether she hadn't sacrificed too much in her quest for stability and her distrust of basic relationships. She'd watched her mother and had sworn from a young age that she'd protect herself from ever getting like that. She'd never let a parade of unsuitable men influence the outcome of her life. She'd never let a weakness for passing fun get the better of her good judgement. She'd never think that salvation could be found at the bottom of a glass or after getting high.

But now it crossed her mind that in her rush to learn her life lessons she'd written off a lot more than just those things.

Had she written off *fun*? Amy pretending to be a domestic goddess for some guy she would get bored with after two minutes...wasn't that *fun*? And how much could you protect yourself from getting hurt? Without becoming a rock, isolated and set apart from the rest of the living, breathing, hurting human race? With John, she'd dipped her toes in the water only to hurriedly yank them out because the temperature hadn't been right. So what happened next? The dry, sterile, clinical life of someone who refused to...*dare*?

'Fine,' Sunny said abruptly, annoyed with herself for the foolish tangent her thoughts had taken. She smiled stiffly and politely. 'I'm sure

Flora will be pleased. What time do you…want me back here or will we be going to somewhere in London? In which case I can meet you both there…'

'Eric will wait for you. Somewhere here, I think. I know a couple of places and it'll be far less tiresome than making the journey into central London, even if Flora and I *can* overnight in my apartment in Mayfair.'

He thought she didn't have fun. Sunny's thoughts were still whirling in her head even though she'd tried to snuff them out with a stern talking-to.

He thought she was an ambitious and probably bitter young woman who didn't know how to do anything else but work. She had no boyfriend, she'd had a sad and challenging life, and now… she worked late every night, did a second job in her free time to earn money and on the weekends caught up on her sleep…when her head wasn't buried in her books.

She recalled him saying that he worked hard but *he played as well…*

She imagined that, deep down, he would expect her to turn up in work clothes if they were going somewhere where the dress code wasn't *jeans and a T-shirt and some trainers.*

Was that why he had kindly warned her that they might be going somewhere *dressy*? Because he feared that she might show up, whatever the occasion, in her stiff little suit and crisp white blouse?

'Okay—' Sunny shrugged '—but I hope he doesn't mind waiting. Girls can be…er…indecisive when it comes to choosing clothes…'

Stefano raised his eyebrows wryly and she flushed because she had the annoying feeling that he could see straight through her—which made her want to carry on protesting.

Yes…girls take time getting their appearance right! And that includes me, whatever you might think!

She was stubbornly determined to prove him wrong and to prove to herself that she hadn't forgotten what it was like to dress up and think of something other than her long-term plans and passing exams.

She'd expected Amy to be horrified at her unexpected arrival but instead the plump, good-natured brunette dimpled smugly and pulled her to one side when she was through the front door.

'The meal was a disaster,' she whispered, giggling. 'Honestly, Sunny, I swear I followed every instruction in the recipe book, more or less, but it was an absolute disaster!'

'Why are you grinning?'

'Because Jake thought it was hilarious! He said he's a brilliant cook and he's been looking for a woman who can be impressed by his culinary skills! Anyway, he's disappeared to the Thai down the road to get us a takeaway and then we're going to watch a movie. You're not *staying*, are you? I mean, that's fine, but would it be awful of me to ask if you could hide out in your bedroom? Just for a bit?'

'I'm not staying!' Sunny laughed. 'But I need you to do me a favour and I need you to do it before Jake gets back with your Thai…because I need your undivided attention…'

Half an hour later, Sunny looked at herself in the full-length mirror in her friend's bedroom.

Her selection of *dressy clothes* was pitiful. She had casual and she had work and then, in between those two polar opposites, she had a paltry array of drab skirts and jumpers that seemed to be neither one thing nor the other.

She'd become accustomed over the years to playing down her looks. Her looks had always earned her the sort of unwarranted attention she'd hated. As far as she was concerned, what mattered was what lay beneath the surface and the only way she had ever felt she could be taken seriously was by muting her appearance. Even when she'd been dating John, dear, thoughtful John, she'd made sure not to dress up. She'd always had the sneaking suspicion that he had been a little threatened and overawed by her appearance and so she had unconsciously accommodated his insecurities.

For the first time, she had the crazy urge to make the absolute most of herself and the only person who could help her was Amy.

Amy had the clothes she lacked and, although they weren't really the same size at all, Amy's clothes were tight, small and stretchy. Many of them were a *one size fits all* variety and Sunny, having had her first few picks ruled out as way too boring for a night out on the town, had allowed herself to be led.

'It's not a *night out on the town*,' she had protested, stepping out of one dress and straight into another. 'His daughter is going to be there!'

'You're going out and it's night time. It's a night out in my book, and he's cute, isn't he? You said so before when I asked.'

'He's full of himself.'

'But cute and sexy.'

'Arrogant and way too...too...*much* for my liking.'

'I notice you didn't dispute the *sexy* bit.' Amy had laughed and spun her round to the full-length mirror.

And now Sunny was staring at the young woman she had spent a lifetime making sure to hide.

Her long slender legs seemed to go on for ever and were on full view in the little stretchy skirt which was a demure pale pink in colour with a far from demure cut. She was taller than her friend, so what would have sat a couple of inches above knee level on Amy just about managed to skim Sunny's thighs.

She had a driving urge to tug the skirt down

and had to squeeze her hands into fists to stop herself from doing it.

The skirt was accompanied by an equally small stretchy top with a scooped neckline and three-quarter length sleeves. Together, she appeared to be wearing a dress, were it not for the fact that when she moved little slivers of her flat belly were exposed.

'Perfect,' Amy declared with satisfaction. 'You have no idea how long I've been wanting to get my hands on you and do this. You can leave your hair the way it is; just run your fingers through it to make it look a little wilder and if you stay still for a couple of seconds I'll put some eyeshadow, mascara and lipgloss on you.' Amy shot her a sly look. 'I must say you're putting yourself out for someone who is *arrogant, full of himself and way too...too...much for your liking...*'

Sunny didn't reply because she was too busy staring at the stranger staring back at her.

Despite the disparity in their height, she and Amy both wore the same shoe size and Sunny had been persuaded into a pair of her friend's shoes which weren't particularly high and weren't particularly flamboyant, at least compared to the revealing outfit, but which still managed to make her look…

Sexy…

She had a sudden attack of panic. She would never, ever have worn anything like this if she'd been going out with girlfriends. She would have been far too terrified of attracting unwanted attention from all the wrong sorts but she would be going out with Stefano and Flora and she was wickedly excited at the prospect of showing him that, yes, she was a fun girl. She was someone who went out, who did all sorts of exciting things in her free time.

She was a sheep in borrowed clothing but he wasn't to know that, was he?

She teamed the outfit with her own denim jacket and hung onto her casual backpack even though Amy did her best to entice her into something small and sparkly.

'You look fab,' her friend said, practically pushing her out of her door because her legs suddenly felt quite leaden. 'Your arrogant dinner date is going to be bowled over! Now, shoo! I have to work on bowling my own dinner date over! Hurry up so that I have time to spray some more perfume and get myself arranged in a way that makes it look as though I haven't been hanging around waiting for him to get back!' Amy smiled and impulsively stood on tiptoe to kiss Sunny on her cheek. 'And have fun, Sunny. You don't do enough of that...'

CHAPTER FIVE

STEFANO STROLLED OVER to the French doors over-
looking the garden and stared in the general direction of the swimming pool. It was darkening
outside, the bright turquoise of the sky fading
into violet and navy. Upstairs, Flora had taken
herself off to change. He hadn't seen her so animated since she had come to live with him. It
wasn't to do with *him* or a sudden interest in de-
veloping a father-daughter relationship. He wasn't
stupid. He knew that. She had been energised by
the excitement of the afternoon because, no matter how surly, grown-up and serious she was, she
was still too young to really appreciate the potential danger Sunny had been in.

He shoved his hand in the pocket of his beige
casual trousers and frowned, recalling every
word she had told him of her unfortunate childhood.

When he had told her that he didn't know every
person working in the law firm, he hadn't been

lying, just as he didn't personally know every single person working in the legal department of his own company, but he knew enough to suspect that the majority of them had not had to struggle to get where they were.

They would mostly be the products of comfortable middle-class families, put through private schools or excellent state schools, brought up on a diet of holidays abroad and generous pocket-money allowances, more than enough to ensure that they didn't have to hold down an extra job in a restaurant to pay the bills.

So what was he to do with this information?

The bottom line was that he fancied her but alongside that elemental physical reaction was the sobering thought that she wasn't like the other women he dated. That, in itself, was inherently disconcerting. Add the relationship she had with his daughter and things moved from disconcerting to downright dangerously foolhardy.

But the more he saw, the more he wanted...

And would she go out with him at all anyway? Was she even interested? Was this physical urge that was making a mockery of his common sense even reciprocated?

She didn't give off all the usual signals. There

were no coy looks or glances held for slightly too long or little-girl helplessness designed to bring out his protective instinct. He didn't know any other woman who would have gone into detail about a miserable, deprived childhood because no one would have seen that as the sort of light-hearted chit-chat which formed part and parcel of verbal foreplay.

And the way she always looked as though she couldn't escape his company fast enough...

She wasn't playing hard to get.

But she blushed...and there were times when there was the ghost of a vibe, some electrical current that he could feel passing between them... soft, subtle, barely there but there enough to make his blood run hot...

Was that why he couldn't seem to get her out of his head? He'd wrapped up his work as quickly as he could earlier today, had delegated a great portion of it to Bob Coombes, one of his CEOs... and he knew he had done that because not only had he wanted to take advantage of the thaw in relations with his daughter, but because he had also wanted to see Sunny.

It was a weakness he didn't care to acknowledge because he allowed himself no weaknesses when it came to women. It didn't matter how sexy a woman was or how much he was interested in bedding her, there was always a part of him that knew he could, in the end, take it or leave it.

He'd never rushed work for any woman before. He hadn't even rushed work for Alicia. In fact, had it not been for the pregnancy, Alicia would have been as temporary as all the women he had dated since his divorce.

But he'd found that he couldn't wait to drive back to the house and surprising her in the swimming pool...

He felt the stirrings of an erection as he recalled the softness of her body against his, the teasing temptation of those stiffened nipples...

Deep in thought, he was hardly aware of Flora until she said, standing in the doorway, 'Sunny's here.'

Stefano smiled, turning. 'You look very pretty, Flora.'

Flora frowned and he wondered whether the fragile truce was over now that Sunny was no longer on the scene as a third party and unwitting mediator.

'No, I don't,' she said bluntly. 'I'm too dark-skinned.'

Stefano looked at her narrowly. 'What on earth are you talking about?'

Flora shrugged and it reminded him of those evasive, dismissive shrugs that Sunny often produced when she had no intention of prolonging a conversation she wasn't interested in having.

Had his daughter picked that up from Sunny? But no…he had noticed that trait before. Were there barely discernible similarities just below the surface, similarities that connected them, explained the way they had just *clicked*? And how could a child who had had it all be similar to a woman who had had nothing as a child?

'Who told you that?' he pressed and was met with another shrug.

'Mum mentioned it now and again.'

'Your mother…' He inhaled deeply and held onto his daughter's serious gaze. 'You're beautiful, Flora, and I'm not just saying that because I'm your…dad…' He had to clear his throat. His voice sounded strangely gruff and he felt a curious lump in his throat when she rolled her eyes but half smiled before leaving the room and heading for the front door.

Dear Alicia, he thought, the corrosive taste of bitterness filling his mouth. She had ensured that their divorce was as acrimonious as possible and, having flown across the ocean with Flora, had made doubly sure that his visiting rights were thwarted at every turn. He had always suspected that she had filled his daughter's head with all sorts of lies and half-truths, even though he had given her every single thing she had requested at the time of the divorce.

But had her machinations gone even further?

Had she taken out her rage and bitterness on their child? Because Flora reminded her of him? Had she made the sort of wilful remarks that had left an impact on Flora? Alicia had been very blonde. He could imagine the ugly twist of her mouth if she'd made a point of criticising Flora's much darker colouring.

If his ex-wife had been standing in front of him right at that very moment, Stefano felt that he would not have been responsible for what he did to her. He could have cheerfully throttled the witch.

Any wonder he'd had his fill of women as long-term investments?

He laughed sourly to himself, heading in his daughter's wake for the front door.

He saw Sunny before she actually saw him because, as he hit the hall, she was turning away, saying something to Eric, laughing.

Stefano stopped dead in his tracks and, eyes narrowed, felt a stab of something like jealousy rip through him.

Gone were the jeans. He'd told her to wear something dressy. He'd expected a variation on her working-clothes theme. Sensible skirt skimming her knees…neat top…camouflage outfit… The sort of nondescript garb designed to make her blend into the background and not draw attention to her stupendous looks.

He knew he'd been guilty of assuming that she was a girl who made it her business to avoid fun, especially after she had told him about her background, especially when he'd connected the pieces and worked out that security was way more important to her than fun, and financial security was really the one thing for which she was quite happy to sacrifice the business of *going out.*

She didn't want to draw attention to herself. He guessed that she'd had a parent who had done that. What she wanted was to fly under the radar, hence her unassuming work clothes and nondescript casual clothes.

She was fiercely independent and to have been

frothy and flirty would have gone against the grain.

He'd made all those sweeping assumptions about her.

She had no boyfriend. Another sweeping assumption was that she wasn't interested in looking for one either. That sort of thing could come later and, when it did, it would be in the form of a serious-minded guy with a stable job, who, like her, wasn't interested in the business of having fun.

It was inexplicable why he was so drawn to her, why she had taken root in his head and why she refused to go.

He liked his women to be fun. The last thing he was interested in was a serious woman because it was a short step between the woman who was serious and the woman who wanted a ring on her finger.

Avoid the serious woman and you avoided the whole ring-on-finger killer conversation.

His mother had always mistakenly imagined that he needed a nice, serious young woman to step into the role of wife and mother. She disapproved of the flighty things who came and went like ships in the night.

He liked the flighty ships in the night, though.

Which was why he'd been frankly bewildered at his reaction to Sunny.

Except...

It seemed some of his assumptions had been wildly off target.

Her long, long hair flowed over her shoulders and down her narrow spine in a tide of unruly but utterly sexy curls, and the outfit...

He broke out in a fine film of perspiration. What happened to the girl who *dressed to hide*? Where the hell had *she* gone? Stefano was almost outraged at the appearance of this sex siren to whom his body was responding with rampant enthusiasm.

He scowled at Eric, who caught his eye, reddened and stepped back just as Sunny turned towards him, all long, long legs and long, long hair, and flashing green eyes.

She should have looked tacky in such a short skirt but the casual denim jacket brought the whole temperature of the outfit down, as did the functional backpack carelessly slung over her shoulder.

Flora was staring at her, mouth open, as though

an alien had suddenly leaped out of the wood-work. Stefano was on her page.

'Did you forget to finish getting dressed?' he heard himself say, moving forward.

It was hardly the sort of compliment she had been expecting and she stiffened, annoyed with herself for having expected any sort of compli-ment at all.

She belatedly wondered whether he was look-ing at the skimpy outfit and wondering what sort of example was being set for Flora.

She swallowed down the urge to tell him that this wasn't her sort of dress code *at all*. Then she remembered what he thought of her, that she was dull, the sort of all-work-and-no-play sort of young woman who had no boyfriend and never went anywhere.

She tilted her chin at a defiant angle and smiled a challenge. 'Not at all,' she chirruped.

'I *love* it,' Flora piped up with gratifying en-thusiasm.

'Thank you very much, Flora!' He might have been sarcastic but she could feel his eyes on her and that dark, intense gaze went to her head like a powerful shot of incense.

'There's not much there to love,' Stefano grated.

'A few square inches of stretchy cloth. I'm surprised you find it comfortable to sit down.'

Actually, she didn't but she wasn't about to tell him that. 'It's…er…what everyone's wearing these days to…er…go out…clubbing…'

'I had no idea you were a clubber,' Stefano muttered disapprovingly, sotto voce, as Flora hopped into the back seat of the car, immediately plugging in her headphones and scrolling through her playlist on her phone.

He was leaning into the car now, his breath warm on her cheek, his dark eyes cool and inscrutable.

'I try and get out whenever I can.' Sunny was beginning to feel horribly uncomfortable in the skimpy outfit, under his accusatory gaze.

What business was it of his anyway? she thought defiantly.

Stefano didn't say anything but he shot a sideways glance at Eric as he slid into the front seat.

He could hardly blame his driver for looking. The outfit was an eye-catcher! She wouldn't be able to walk five steps without drawing stares. Should he revisit his choice of restaurant? Perhaps stay at the house and have one of the caterers he used come in and do the honours? He'd thought of the restaurant in question because it often attracted minor celebrities and he'd thought that might be fun for Flora. Now he had visions of tacky minor celebrities ogling Sunny, maybe trying to slip her their number.

He couldn't even kid himself that he was taking an avuncular interest in her well-being, protecting her from male attention she didn't like. No. He didn't want men staring at her and thinking about making passes because he wanted her for himself. Didn't matter how hard he fought it, that was the base line, wasn't it? He wanted her.

They covered the short distance to the restaurant in silence. Sunny stared through the window while next to her Flora was in a world of her own, listening to music.

When she glanced down, she could see way too much thigh exposed because the skirt had ridden up. He'd seen her in a bikini, had already seen a lot more of her body than was on show now, but this felt *different*.

Not that he was looking. Except in a derogatory way.

She was unusually quiet over the meal, only interacting when pulled into the conversation. The food was delicious and the crowd was interesting. Flora, for once showing her age, got a little excited and bright-eyed at seeing a boy who was, she whispered, the lead singer in a boy band, the name of which neither she nor Stefano recognised.

Wearing this outfit had been a crazy idea. She'd wanted to prove something and the only thing she'd proved was that she had it in her to be just like her mother. Her mother used to dress like this—*worse*, tiny little clothes that left nothing to the imagination and attracted all the wrong attention from all the wrong men.

The more she thought of that, the worse she felt. Instead of seeing her in a different light, Stefano would now see her as someone cheap and easy, someone who stopped being a lawyer the second she could wriggle out of her suit. She worked so hard to project the image she wanted the world to see that it was horrible suspecting that one impulsive decision might have left him with the wrong impression of her.

They stayed at the restaurant far longer than she had expected. Flora, animated and excited at seeing the very young-looking boy band member, dragged her meal out for as long as she could and then insisted on having dessert.

'Why don't you stay the night?' Stefano suggested, turning to look at her from the front seat.

An exhausted Flora had ended up half asleep on Sunny's shoulder but she roused herself sufficiently to sleepily agree with the suggestion.

'It's Sunday tomorrow so, unless you have plans, stay over and have another day out here. It's far nicer than being in London and you can try your hand at swimming again, if you haven't been scared off...'

'Thank you,' Sunny said politely, 'but I couldn't possibly.'

'Why not?'

'Because...' There were a lot of reasons to choose from. *How about*, she wanted to say, *because you make me feel uncomfortable and just the thought of being under the same roof as you overnight sends shivers down my spine? How about the fact that I don't have a change of clothes and I'll die if I have to spend another day in these?* And his suggestion that she try her hand at swimming again? Well, Sunny wanted to laugh out loud at that because there was no way that she was going to parade in her bikini in front of him.

'You heard Flora. She'd like it. Wouldn't you, Flora?'

'I don't think it's very fair to try and coerce your daughter into siding with you.'

'I can play dirty if the occasion demands... Think about it.' He turned back around and within minutes the car was pulling through the stone pillars that heralded the long drive up to the house.

Flora was dead on her feet and was in bed within half an hour and, since it seemed rude to disappear without thanking him properly for the meal, Sunny hovered, feeling more and more conspicuous in the wretched outfit.

'Well? What's your decision to be?' He'd re-appeared through one of the side doors, having obviously gone somewhere else after he had dropped his daughter to her bedroom.

Sunny feasted her eyes on him. He hadn't dressed formally for the meal and was wearing a simple pair of black trousers and a cream linen shirt which highlighted his wildly exotic bronzed skin tone. All at once several thoughts raced through her head, clamouring for attention.

'I have a lot to do tomorrow,' she began back-tracking but in her head all she could think about was…those fabulous dark eyes coolly assessing her in her borrowed clothes, coolly making judgements, coolly sneering at her.

All her dormant insecurities, ones she had thought she had put to rest a long time ago, wriggled out of their shallow graves.

She remembered the men who had come and gone, chasing behind her mother…she remembered the way her foster father's eyes had followed her even though she had dressed like a nun in his presence…she remembered the boys she had met at boarding school, the way *they* had looked, as though their fingers were itching to touch…

She remembered the way she had never quite managed to fit in, always standing out amongst those well-bred girls with their braying laughs and bone-deep self-confidence.

She thought that if one of that type had dressed in a short skirt and top Stefano would never have dreamed of making awful sarcastic remarks at her expense.

If, say, Katherine had worn an outfit which, quite honestly, was hardly anything out of the ordinary on a girl in her early twenties, Stefano would probably have *complimented* her on it, rather than asking whether she had forgotten to finish putting on her clothes.

'I resent the way you insulted me,' she heard herself burst out.

She honestly hadn't meant to say anything and she couldn't imagine why she had because that sort of remark was a glaring admission of her insecurities—insecurities she didn't want to advertise. Not to him, not to anyone.

Stefano, thrown a curve ball, stared at her in frowning silence.

'Explain,' he said eventually. 'And sit while you explain. You make me feel like a kid called into the principal's office to account for himself.' He turned away and poured them both a glass of wine. They had only drunk a small amount at dinner, which had seemed a good idea with Flora present, and right now he felt as if he needed to make up for the oversight. 'How have I insulted you?' He sat down and dragged a chair over with his foot, pushing it back slightly so that he could extend his long legs on it as a foot rest.

The joys of great wealth, Sunny thought, without a trace of envy but more than a hint of stark realism. Every stick of furniture in the kitchen was handmade. It was obvious. You could feel it in the solidity of the wood and the smoothness of the grain. However, it would never have occurred to Stefano to be precious around any of the furniture because if it got scratched or even destroyed, it could all be replaced with the click of an imperious finger.

'My outfit,' she muttered, already regretting having brought this grievance out into the open because, the second she mentioned what she was wearing, his dark, lazy eyes obligingly roamed over her body, bringing her out in a tingle of excruciating awareness.

'What about it?' Had she noticed the way men had stared covertly at her when they had walked into the airy dining room? Flora would have been mortified had she only noticed that the underage boy-band member had done his fair share of staring at Sunny. Stefano had noticed it all and he hadn't liked any of it.

He'd never cared what the women he dated wore. Indeed, most of them wore less than Sunny was wearing now, hadn't thought twice about displaying their wares, just so that he could be in no doubt as to what he was getting.

Had he ever felt the slightest inclination to demand that any of them change their clothes?

Dress in something prissier? Something, preferably, that covered from neck to ankle?

Simple answer…no.

But he'd had to bite back the urge to hurry the meal along this evening so that he could remove an oblivious Sunny from the sideways glances she was commanding from every single male in the room with a pulse.

He could only assume that he was so accustomed to getting exactly what he wanted, when he wanted it, from the opposite sex, that her lack of availability was stirring all sorts of puzzling responses in him. Responses that were unwanted and definitely out of bounds!

Not only was she not making any moves to attract his attention, but she was actively discouraging it.

And it wasn't, as he had assumed, that she actively discouraged *all male attention*. If she did, then she surely wouldn't own an outfit like the one she was wearing.

'I didn't appreciate your insinuating that I looked like…like a tart.' Her voice was barely audible and she was beetroot red, but it had to be said. Considering she'd begun.

Stefano flushed darkly because he could hardly

try and adopt a pious stance when he knew exactly what she was talking about.

Even if she *had* managed to misconstrue the intention behind his words.

'I thought you might have been uncomfortable with the sort of unwarranted attention an outfit like that might attract.'

'I'm not wearing anything any girl in her twenties might not wear.'

'But not many of them have the sort of knockout figure to do justice to it...'

Sunny blinked and then, as the full meaning of his words sank in, she felt her whole body react with just the slightest of trembles. Because those words, huskily spoken, seemed to target every single inappropriate thought she had had about him, ripping them free of the innocent labels she had done her best to attach to them.

He wasn't making a pass at her, she told herself firmly. Maybe he was flirting but, if he was, then he was on a road to nowhere because she didn't do flirting! Especially with someone like Stefano Gunn!

But he'd thrown her off course and she was having trouble marshalling her thoughts.

Stefano watched the way she stiffened, straightening her narrow shoulders. She wasn't quite meeting his eyes, but her mouth had tightened and her expression was shuttered and she was perched on the edge of her chair as though making sure she could leap out of it as fast as possible, should the situation demand.

'I apologise if you found my comment about your outfit...offensive,' he offered gruffly. 'And you're absolutely right, of course. You aren't wearing anything that any other girl your age wouldn't wear. In fact, I know a few who would cheerfully wear half as much and they're twice your age...'

Sunny relaxed a little. She stared at the glass of wine, as if only noticing it for the first time, and took a tentative sip.

Now she felt as if she might have overreacted. He'd hit a nerve, but how was he supposed to have known that? She was struck by another thought...

Had he made that remark, spontaneously and without thinking, because he had felt that she would not have *blended in* with the crowd in the posh restaurant he had taken them to? Had he thought that she would stick out like a sore thumb amongst the upper-middle-class suburban crowd with their cardigans and pearls? When he'd told her that he'd only been thinking about her and the unwarranted attention she might have been exposed to, had he really been saying that he'd been thinking about himself and his embarrassment at being seen with someone who clearly didn't know the dress code for the expensive restaurant he had taken them to…?

In truth, she'd barely noticed who was there at all. She'd been too busy feeling self-conscious. But of course it would have been a wealthy crowd.

A fresh wave of insecurity washed over her, ebbing to leave a sour taste at the back of her mouth.

Now he was being *kind* and she hated that.

'I only reacted because…'

'Because…?'

'My mother used to dress in skimpy clothes,' Sunny burst out, inwardly groaning at the lack of control that seemed to sweep over her whenever he was around. It was as if he could somehow get her to say stuff she wouldn't normally say and he could get her to do that without even trying. She feverishly played with the stem of her wine glass with frowning concentration. 'I always swore that I would never dress in anything that wasn't...wasn't...'

'Buttoned up to the neck? That didn't cover as much as possible without inviting heatstroke...?'

'She had no control,' Sunny said helplessly. 'In and out of drink and drugs and guys...' She felt tears of self-pity sting the back of her eyes and she wanted the ground to open and swallow her up. 'You have no idea...' she said in a muffled voice.

She was hardly aware of him leaving his seat so that he could drag a chair close to her. She was grateful for her hair, which hung across her cheeks, shielding her expression.

'I'm sorry,' Stefano said with urgent sincerity. He reached out to stroke the side of her face and then gently tilted it so that she was looking at him. This was so inappropriate and yet it felt so *right*. He thought about all the reasons why he shouldn't be touching her at all, not even the most innocent of touches, of which this definitely wasn't one, and all that emerged was the stark ferocity of his physical response. It seemed to batter through everything to emerge the victor.

'These aren't even my clothes,' Sunny whispered, even though she had told herself that there was no way she would admit to that because she had been so keen to prove to him that she was capable of *having fun* just like any other girl her age.

'No?' Stefano wondered why he was so relieved to hear that. Her skin, under the roughened pad of his thumb, was velvety-smooth and her eyes, up close like this, were the clearest green he had ever seen, the colour of sea-washed glass.

'They belong to the girl I share the flat with,' Sunny confessed, resisting the urge to lean into the gentle absent-minded strokes of his finger on her cheek. Her heart was racing. This felt very, very dangerous but she told herself that that was purely in her imagination because he was just being kind.

And she didn't want him to be kind... She wanted him to be...a man...

Her breathing became shallow and her eyelids fluttered as the realisation settled like a leaden weight in the pit of her stomach. Finding him attractive had been inexplicable enough but at least that had been a passive situation, something she could deal with, even if it was inconvenient.

But wanting him to carry on touching her *all*

over, wanting him to look at her with the hunger of a man looking at a woman he wanted…

She eased back and immediately missed the headiness of being close to him and feeling his skin against hers.

'Amy lent them to me,' she said in a more matter-of-fact voice. 'She thought they might look a bit better than the usual stuff I wear when I go out…'

After that brief moment of intimacy, Stefano could feel her pulling away from him and the need to recapture the lost connection slammed into him with the force of a freight train.

'But I didn't feel comfortable in them, if you want to know the truth.' She gave a careless shrug, hoping to dispel the electric charge between them.

A girl could lose herself in his eyes, she thought a little wildly. So it was no wonder that she was falling victim to all sorts of wobbly legs type feelings!

'Why the name?' Stefano murmured before she could slip away into polite conversation, before she could distance herself from him.

'I beg your pardon?'

'Your name. Is it a nickname? Because, from

what you've told me about yourself…about your mother…'

'You're not really interested in that!' Sunny laughed weakly. 'And I'm sorry for being such a wimp and spilling my guts out! I'm sure that's not the sort of thing you bargained for when you asked me to come along with you and Flora tonight…' Hot and bothered by the way he was looking at her, she tried to find something sensible to say about Flora, some observation that would turn the intimacy of this conversation around because her bones were melting, especially because, instead of taking the hint and pulling away from her after she had tactfully drawn back, he had sat forward, once again closing the distance between them.

Nothing sensible came to mind and she licked her lips nervously.

'I'm interested,' Stefano murmured.

Sunny sighed. No big deal. Was it…?

'She was in one of her optimistic windows,' she said sadly. 'That's what she told me many times over the years. She'd come off the drugs and the drink as soon as she found out that she was pregnant with me…'

'And your father?'

Sunny lowered her eyes and felt her breath catch. 'No idea. Probably just another drifter...'

'I'm sorry.'

And he sounded as though he genuinely meant that, which brought a lump to her throat. Her eyes tangled with his and clung. He had, she thought distractedly, the most wickedly long eyelashes...

'You were saying...' Stefano reminded her.

'So I was. I was saying that Mum was off the bad stuff and she just plucked the most hopeful name she could think of...' Sunny smiled wryly '...and I've been stuck with it ever since. I haven't even got a useful middle name I could have reverted to...'

'Your outfit,' Stefano murmured.

Sunny tensed. 'I can't wait to get it off...'

'I didn't say...what I said to be insulting...'

'Maybe you thought I wouldn't fit in with that crowd.' She forestalled any truths that she knew would cut to the quick.

He looked at her with open puzzlement and she laughed, knowing that she'd at least got that bit wrong. He wasn't the sort to care what other people thought.

'I said what I said because...' he sat back and folded his arms, his eyes not wavering '...the thought of other men looking at you...' He shouldn't be doing this but knowing that didn't help and didn't change anything. He was experiencing that very, very rare feeling of being at the mercy of something bigger and more powerful than his own iron willpower. He allowed his words to sink in, not knowing whether she would respond at all but driven to find out because he *just had to.* 'Well, put it this way... I didn't like the idea and I couldn't see how they could fail to stare in that outfit of yours...'

'You didn't like the idea...' She felt as if she was suddenly walking through thick fog with no signposts in sight.

'Men look...and then they want...' He shrugged in a way that was typically foreign, an overblown gesture that seemed to convey dry amusement and impatient resignation at the same time. 'I didn't like the thought of that...'

'Of what?'

'Of both...' His stomach clenched because, for once, he wasn't staring at a guaranteed outcome. She was quirky and...unpredictable, and both those things added up, for him, to an unknown quantity. And for once the riptide was carrying him. He didn't like it or want it but he was powerless to resist it.

'I didn't like the thought of them looking…and I didn't like the thought of them wanting…I felt that both those things should come from…me…'

CHAPTER SIX

SUNNY STARED AT Stefano in wide-eyed bewilderment, certain that she had somehow got the wrong end of the stick.

'What are you saying?' she stammered.

'Surely I don't have to spell it out in words of one syllable.' His voice was husky and teasing but that thread of uncertain apprehension was still pouring through his veins, investing him with the sort of edge-of-seat feeling he had never had much time for.

His edge-of-seat feelings were all associated with times he would rather not have remembered. The edge-of-seat feelings of waiting for lawyers to try and make progress with resolving custody issues...the edge-of-seat feelings of knowing that his marriage had been a crashing mistake, a disaster that would have to be put right with a messy divorce...the edge-of-seat feelings that had always come whenever he had tried to gain access to see his daughter, half optimistic that this time his ex-wife wouldn't mess him around, half accepting that she probably would...

Catastrophes, he had reflected on more than one bitter occasion, had a way of sharpening up and clarifying the way you looked at things.

Stefano no longer welcomed anything in his life that couldn't be ruthlessly controlled. No situation was ever allowed to deviate from the course he determined. No one was ever allowed to overstep the boundaries he had laid down. And he never allowed himself to flounder... Ever...

Steer a clear route, make sure you didn't stray from it, and nothing could take you by surprise because surprises were seldom good.

Except, right now, the clear route wasn't as clear as it usually was, when it came to women.

For starters, he had chased her. Not overtly, but did that make a difference? He had noted her Keep Off signs and, instead of shrugging and walking away because the world was full of pretty faces and willing women, he had let himself be hooked in.

He had changed his routine because of her. Having hired her to work nights so that he could focus on several high-powered deals that required long hours, he had caught himself thinking about her, wanting to see her for longer than just in passing...

And when he had shown up unexpectedly and found her in the swimming pool...

That modest black bikini, which was much more her thing than the outfit she had borrowed from her friend, had turned him on more than if she had been wearing nothing but a thong...

Which just went to show the power of the imagination once it broke its leash and decided to fly. He'd been determined not to go near her, to remember that she was connected with his daughter, to not under any circumstances *mix business with pleasure*, so to speak, and yet here he was... Hell, he'd resolved not to venture *near* her in case it jeopardised his fragile truce with Flora...!

Not even her cautionary tale about her background had put him off.

It should have.

He had married a gold-digger and paid the price. Now he had no problem dating beauties who enjoyed the things he could give them, but he was always in control of a relationship, always dictated its course, always dispatched them when they were beginning to outstay their welcome.

Sunny had no money and her background beggared belief. She kept her distance and had made it clear that, given the choice, she would not have chosen to be in his company if she could help it. And yet…he had still chased her.

Which said worrying things about his valued self-control…but he was incapable of backing off. He didn't get it. He didn't *begin* to get it.

Something about the way she was put together… It wasn't just her stupendous and unusual good looks, but the way she tried to conceal them. It wasn't just her sharp intellect, but the soft vulnerability he could see lurking just beneath it. She had somehow gained access to Flora, a feat none of his previous nannies had come close to accomplishing, and she had done so without trying, having made it very clear that she was only in it for the money, which she needed.

On paper, it made no sense for him to be sitting here, waiting for her to come on board with the little journey he was interested in taking with her…

But hell…since when was it written in cement that he had to follow the rules that made sense?

Since when was a little deviation something to be banned? And he wouldn't be jeopardising anything. He knew what could be lost and so would also know how to avoid that happening. He'd admitted his own weakness and stepped back to see the situation from all angles.

When it came to the crunch, he would always be in control because that was just the man he was. His concerns, whilst valid, were misplaced. To know what you were dealing with was to be in charge of the situation. He knew what he was dealing with. An itch that begged to be scratched and, once scratched, would disappear. It was a relief to get that straight in his head.

'I fancy you,' he admitted with a slow smile that sent her senses spinning. It was liberating not to be fighting the unequal fight any longer. 'Don't ask me why but I do...'

Sunny felt as though she were being stroked even though he hadn't laid a finger on her. Her tummy flipped over and for a second every principle she had held dear to her heart disappeared like water down a plughole.

She shook away the mesmeric effect his words were having on her to establish some sanity.

He fancied her!

She'd been fancied before, she scoffed. True, Stefano Gunn was a few notches higher than most but still...

Agitated, she clasped her hands together and looked away. All of that would have been easy to deal with if she didn't, likewise, fancy the man!

'Could the outfit have anything to do with your sudden attack of lust?' She was proud of the casual, dismissive tone of her voice, which didn't seem to have the slightest effect on him.

'Not at all,' Stefano said musingly, as though he'd considered her question and given it a lot of thought. 'Although, in fairness, it did concentrate matters when I realised that I didn't want other men seeing you wearing next to nothing.'

'Well, I... This isn't at all appropriate...' She wanted to stand up but he was sitting so close to her that she would have had to push him back and then clamber over him.

She shrank back as far as she could go into her chair and noted the mild amusement in his eyes when he looked at her.

Why did she have to fancy him? Of all people? Why did those physical responses, which she had assumed she lacked, have to jump out and target a man like Stefano Gunn?

Why couldn't they have targeted someone nice and kind and *ordinary*?

Her skin tingled and prickled with awareness. Now that she knew how he felt, it was as if a Pandora's box had been opened. The silent, shameful charge, which she had thought had just been about her, was out in the open and it was clamouring to be dealt with.

'Tell me why,' Stefano murmured, his antennae picking up her nerves and processing it. She wasn't saying anything he didn't privately think himself but such caution didn't stand a chance next to the demands of his wayward libido.

'Because...I happen to be working for you!'

'In a very temporary capacity,' Stefano dismissed drily. 'I'm not your boss and you're not my employee and there are no office politics to be dealt with.'

'Of course there would be office politics to be dealt with! Not that I intend to...to...to *do anything.*'

'What office politics?'

'This is crazy.' She stood up, nimbly avoiding crashing into him by a whisker and then there was an awkward few seconds while she hovered, waiting for him to shift away from her and wondering whether he intended to at all, before he moved and she slipped past to pace the kitchen floor.

She should go. Of course she should! But something was holding her back, weakening what her head was telling her to do. Temptation. This was what it felt like. She had never experienced it in her life before and after John, who had been just the sort of guy she should have felt tempted by, she had resigned herself to her future being about her career. She felt uncomfortable in her own skin, confused by having her neatly ordered life turned upside down.

'What office politics?'

She paused to stand in front of him, arms folded, mouth pursed. 'You know what I'm talking about!'

'I have no idea and I'm not a mind-reader. If there's some revelation I've been missing, then enlighten me...'

'Katherine,' she muttered, hating herself for what now sounded like office gossip. She couldn't even remember where this particular piece of office gossip had originated.

'Katherine?' His brows knitted into a perplexed frown.

'Nothing. Forget it. It's nothing.'

'You shouldn't start conversations you don't have the courage to finish.' He'd never had to work so hard for a woman. It was as though she had glanced over her shoulder, thrown him a half smile and then proceeded to lay down a bed of nails and burning embers over which he had to walk if he was to follow the glance and the half smile. And where would he get even if he followed the glance and the half smile?

Nowhere much. He wasn't interested in a full-blown relationship. She turned him on and her unattainability was even more of a turn-on but he knew that the second he had her they would both be at the beginning of the end. Since his messy divorce and the bitter disillusionment that had come with it, he had had neither the will nor the stamina to sustain any liaison beyond a couple of months. He didn't jump out of bed with one woman to immediately jump into bed with another, but even after periods of celibacy, sometimes lasting months, he had never had the desire for any relationship with any woman to go beyond its natural course. Which was limited.

So it was puzzling why he was so keen to pursue something that would have a very limited duration.

Sunny could have kicked herself for ever having mentioned Katherine, but wasn't this the man he was? Sexy…powerful…wealthy…a man who thought he could chase whatever woman caught his fancy?

For all she knew, Katherine might have been busy this evening and so he'd thought he'd chance it with her.

That didn't sit quite right but it felt good not to give him the benefit of the doubt.

Because she wasn't going to go to bed with him. It didn't matter whether she fancied him or not or whether he fancied her or not. Did it?

'What about Katherine?' he prompted. 'Are you concerned that if we sleep together, she'll find out and sack you?'

'We're *not* going to be sleeping together!'

But they were. Stefano could read the conflict inside her as if it had been written in neon lettering across her forehead and he felt a kick of pure masculine triumph.

Was this just about winning? He'd never thought of sex in those terms. But, then again, he'd never met a woman who hadn't been eager and willing to fall into bed with him…

'I won't tell if you don't…' he murmured.

Sunny wondered whether he'd just heard what she'd said. His rampant self-confidence was a treacherous turn-on even though she should have found it repellent. She tilted her chin defiantly. 'It's not about whether Katherine finds out…it's just that I wouldn't want to step on any toes…'

'What are you talking about?'

'The rumour mill has it that the only reason the company got your business was because of Katherine…'

'Is that a fact…?'

'I don't suppose I should be telling you any of this, but I just want to make you see why this is crazy and why…well…why…'

'Now you've started telling me…what it is that you shouldn't be telling me…perhaps you should finish… What about Katherine? What's that rumour mill been saying?'

Hoist by my own petard, was what sprang to Sunny's mind. She hated gossip and yet here she was, repeating it. She couldn't even pretend that it was illuminating work-related gossip, gossip that Stefano might find useful or that he needed to know.

It was cheap tabloid gossip and she cringed with shame but he was looking at her narrowly, waiting for her to carry on. She couldn't suddenly change the subject and start talking about the weather or the state of the economy.

'I don't usually listen to gossip—*I don't*—but it's been impossible to get away from. The minute everyone found out that you were going to be using Marshall, Jones and Jones, the speculation began because…it's new on the scene and it's small. It's not one of the top five…which is where…you know, one might assume…well…' She heard herself tripping over her words and she took a deep breath because now that she'd started this stupid, idiotic story she was committed to finish it.

'One might indeed…' Stefano murmured. He had no time for gossip and even less time for people who had nothing better to do than to spread it but he found the agonising discomfort on her face made her seem impossibly young and vulnerable, especially because she was desperately trying to keep her cool.

He also believed her when she said that she

didn't usually listen to gossip. Where two or more people were gathered, gossip became an inevitability and, in a work environment, it was almost impossible to escape it.

Unless, of course, you happened to live in an ivory tower, which, as the head of his sprawling empire, he more or less did.

'So the rumour started that…that…perhaps Katherine was at the heart of it…'

Stefano raised his eyebrows, amazed that wagging tongues could have struck jackpot with nothing to go on but pure speculation. 'Explain,' he said with undisguised curiosity.

Sunny allowed herself a little sigh of relief because at least he wasn't storming around the kitchen, threatening to have her sacked because since when was it part of her job description to gossip to the guy who would be bringing tens of thousands of pounds' worth of business to their company.

'Katherine's very beautiful and someone came to the conclusion that you might have handed some work to the company as a way of…of… of…'

'Shall I help you along with this?'

Sunny stared at him miserably. She wanted

to tell him that that *someone* who had come to conclusions hadn't been *her*. She had no idea whether the conclusions were right or wrong, but she hated the thought that he might end up being contemptuous of her. Too much protesting of her innocence, however, would surely end up not ringing true.

'You think,' Stefano said helpfully, 'that I wanted to climb into bed with the very beautiful Katherine and my method of getting her to go along with that was via bringing business to the company...'

'Stupid,' Sunny muttered, mortified.

'A little insulting,' Stefano mused. He thought his mother might have been highly entertained at what her machinations had instigated. 'I mean,' he said softly, 'don't you think that I might, just might, be perfectly capable of wooing the very beautiful Katherine without having to exert a bribe...?'

'I have no idea how that rumour started.' She tried not to fidget in her acute discomfort.

How on earth had they got to this point anyway? It wasn't as though she was going to jump in the sack with him! And yet, if that were the case, shouldn't she just have laughed off his crazy proposition and headed for the door?

It was what any normal, disinterested and frankly appalled person might have done...

Perhaps not appalled, she mentally amended. Who would be appalled at having a pass made at them by Stefano Gunn? He was sex on legs and probably the most eligible bachelor in the country, if not on the planet.

'Although...' he stood up, flexed his muscles and paced the kitchen, finally pouring them both another glass of wine '... I'll admit there's a certain amount of truth behind the rumour so whoever started it must have heard something...'

Sunny felt her insides plummet. She had been shocked when he had told her that he fancied her and she knew that she must have played with the idea of sleeping with him, must have entertained the wicked thought in some small corner of her mind, because to hear him now confirm that Katherine had been the draw for him made her feel slightly queasy.

Had she turned him down? And had his eyes wandered a little further afield until they had alighted on *her*?

'It's none of my business,' she said crisply,

standing up so that he got the message that she was leaving.

'Where are you going?'

'Home. It's late.'

'I don't want you to go.'

'Tough.'

'Do you?'

'Do I what?'

'Want to go?' He watched her as she hovered by the door, saw the flicker of indecision on her face, saw the way she took a deep breath, as though steeling herself to clear off. 'I would never make a pass at a woman and then, if I happen to get rejected, scout around for someone else to pick up the slack. I'm not that superficial, Sunny. I don't want Katherine, however beautiful and capable she might be. And I'll tell you something for free...shall I?'

'What?' *He didn't want Katherine. He didn't fancy her.* Relief shot through her and in that moment she knew that she wanted him, that it didn't make sense, not at all, but something in her wanted him and that something was far more powerful than the neat, tidy part of her brain that was telling her not to be a fool.

'What I'm doing right now,' Stefano drawled,

his deep, velvety voice curling around her with the seductiveness of the richest, darkest, smoothest chocolate, 'is not what I usually do. I don't usually make passes at women. I don't usually lay my cards on the table and try to persuade a woman to share my bed. But something about you...'

Sunny was beginning to feel faint. 'If you don't fancy Katherine, then what did you mean when you said that there was truth to the rumour...?' She was struggling to think straight because all of a sudden her head was filled with the most erotic images, images that had never formed a part of her life at all. Images of her making love...giving in with wild abandon to a deep vein of passion she had never known existed in her.

Stefano grinned ruefully and she blinked because he no longer looked like the intimidating, ruthless tycoon that he was. He looked *sexy and tantalisingly approachable.*

'I have my mother to thank for engineering my association with your company.'

'Not *my* company,' Sunny automatically said in a distracted voice.

Stefano smiled. 'True. My mother...' he raked his fingers through his hair because this was as intimate a chat with a woman as he could remember having in a very long time indeed '...has taken it upon herself to try and find me a nice wife ever since my daughter came to live with me after Alicia died. She's of the opinion that a girl needs a mother and, in passing, a wife would do me good.'

'Oh...'

'Oh, indeed,' Stefano said wryly. 'When my mother puts her mind to something, she can be a force of nature. She gets convenient hearing loss when I try and explain to her that a wife isn't going to happen.' He hadn't envisaged, when he'd put forward his bold proposal, that he would end up explaining any of this to her but, now that he was, he thought that it might be a good idea.

He'd always made it clear to the women he slept with that he wasn't up for grabs. There wouldn't be long-range plans or meet and greet the relatives or any talk at all about a future that wasn't going to be on the cards.

If any of them decided that they could somehow find a way past those clear, simple clauses then they were destined for disappointment.

But then all those women had been eager and enthusiastic. Sunny hadn't been either of those things and, more importantly, she'd also managed to charm his wilful daughter.

It was doubly important that she didn't see any relationship they might have as a gateway to something meaningful because of her connection to Flora.

Would she anyway? He just didn't know. What he *did* know was that, underneath the veneer, she was peculiarly vulnerable because of her background.

He wondered how it was that he knew so much about her when he hadn't slept with her. He wondered whether instant sexual gratification had always obviated the need for meaningful personal conversations or whether his interest in her had been sparked by the fact that his daughter was part of the equation. Somehow, through her association with Flora, she had managed to find a back door into parts of him no other woman had managed to access after the bitter fallout of his marriage. Was this something that had made him curiously vulnerable to the thought of bedding her? Had the very thing that should have deterred him been the match that had lit the burning flame?

He wondered whether Alicia, the mother of his

child, had ever had any real access to him or whether their doomed relationship had generated something that had seemed personal at the time but which, in retrospect, had just been the sort of intimacy that warring partners sometimes had. Intimacy of the wrong kind.

The roundabout cycle of pointless questions was irritating and he focused on the here and now.

'She knows Katherine's mother,' he elaborated with a shrug, 'and she promptly decided that a love match was on the cards.'

'And you went along with it?' Sunny was puzzled because that element of softness was not what she associated with him.

The conversation seemed to be getting more rather than less personal and Stefano hesitated before dismissing the distant sound of alarm bells ringing.

'I am close to my mother,' he told her neutrally. 'I may not agree with her efforts to find me a suitable bride but I thought that it would cost nothing to place some of my business with your company and meet the woman, rather than staging a flat-out refusal and upsetting my mother, who, at the end of the day, is just doing what she feels is best for myself and my daughter. Naturally, I did all the necessary checks to ensure that the company was capable of delivering what I wanted of them. I wasn't about to sacrifice my money for the sake of my mother's whimsy.'

'Naturally.' Sunny cleared her throat. If he had gone full-steam ahead and tried to seduce her with his sheer overwhelming physicality she would have resisted, or at least she *hoped* that she would have resisted. Instead, they were talking and she got the feeling that she had, for whatever reason, been allowed into an inner circle to which not many were invited. She had no idea where that impression came from. Maybe because underneath the casual tone of his voice there was something ever so slightly…hesitant. As though he was picking his words carefully because he was in foreign territory.

It was fanciful, of course. For all she knew, this could be a tried and tested ruse to get what he wanted. State his intentions…switch tactics to persuasive conversation…then stake his claim… It helped to be cynical but not even that could kill her curiosity.

'Your parents must have a very close marriage,' she said wistfully. 'I've always thought that people who are happily married are the ones who recommend marriage...'

'My father's dead but yes, they had a very happy marriage.' He was bemused at the twists and turns their conversation was taking, whilst telling himself that exchanging a few personal details wasn't anything of earth-shattering importance, even if those personal details were not ones he'd ever exchanged with the women who had flitted in and out of his life in the past few years.

'Girls need a mother—' Sunny thought of her own mother and all her tragic failings and she thought of all the allowances she had made for her '—so maybe your mother has a point.' She shrugged, just in case he thought that she was overstepping the mark in giving an opinion.

'In an ideal world—' Stefano thought that this might be the perfect opportunity to get a few things straight '—Flora would have a delightful and adoring mummy, but it isn't an ideal world. A delightful and adoring mummy would necessitate me having a wife and that's a country I've visited once and have no intention of returning to.' He drained his glass, stood up, strolled towards the wide windows that overlooked the extensive back lawns before turning to face her. 'I've been married once,' he said flatly, 'and it was an unmitigated disaster. That's something I need not tell you, but it might explain why there is no Katherine on the face of the earth who could entice me back into thinking that marriage is anything but a train wreck waiting to happen.'

'That's very cynical.'

'You think? I'm surprised we don't share the same sentiment.'

'You mean because of…my background?'

'Yes.' Stefano was curious enough to prolong the conversation. 'Surely you can't tell me that you believe in fairy stories and happy endings when your mother was, from all accounts, a failed and unhappy woman and your father… was a bloke who did a runner before you were born and never looked back…?'

Sunny flushed. He wasn't pulling any punches, was he? But there was nothing disdainful or pitying about his remarks. He was saying it like it was and, weirdly, she didn't seem to mind that.

'I've never thought about it one way or the other.' She felt the nervous beat of the pulse at the base of her neck. His eyes resting lazily on her seemed like the whisper of a promise of things to come and every nerve in her body was on full alert, throbbing with barely contained excitement.

'Are you asking me that because you want to warn me not to get involved with you?'

Stefano shot her a curling smile because there was unspoken acquiescence in that question, although he was certain that she barely realised that herself.

'I'm not looking for involvement with anyone,' Sunny dismissed. She glanced jumpily at him and licked her lips, which were dry and tingly. 'And maybe you're right. Maybe I'm not really interested and haven't actually thought about it because of my background.' She gave him a sad, twisted smile. 'Maybe it's because I don't exactly have the right role models to fall back on. How could I believe in fairy tales and happy endings when I never knew what that sort of thing was like in the first place? Maybe you just can't crave what you've never had or experienced.' She wasn't sure whether she really believed that or not. She knew that when she'd thought she'd found her soulmate she had desperately *wanted* the happy-ever-after ending except the soulmate hadn't quite worked out as planned.

Since then, had she toughened up? Turned into the sort of cynical career woman who had no time for love and romance?

She'd thought she'd given up on having the sort of capacity for a physical response that was necessary for any sort of relationship, but she was wrong, wasn't she? Turned out she did have the capacity for a physical response…

So was she kidding herself that she never thought about the future and what it might hold for her with a guy? Should the right guy come along one day?

If Stefano was warning her off getting ideas about him, as if that would ever happen in a million years, then to tell him that, for all the chaos and heartache of her background, she still believed in the enduring power of love would be a mistake.

He'd get cold feet and run a mile and—why kid herself?— she didn't want that.

'You don't have to warn me off,' she said huskily, daring to step into the unknown and feeling a shiver of molten excitement, 'because, like I said, the last thing I would want would be involvement…' She laughed, heady with the sensation that she was no longer talking to the formidable, feared and respected Stefano Gunn, the man who could make heads of finance quake in their shoes, whose ability to close deals and predict the stock market swings was legendary, who could command immediate attention with the snap of his fingers...

She was talking to a man who fancied her and right now she was no longer the junior in a law firm in the presence of the toughest guy in the concrete jungle. They were both adults working their way towards sleeping with one another.

It was...*thrilling*. It made her realise how predictable her life was. She had spent so long making sure to impose order and control, so that she would never have a runaway future, that somehow the present had become lost in the process, as had *fun*.

'And especially involvement with a guy like you,' she completed with utter honesty.

Stefano, relieved as he was to know that they were both singing from the same song sheet, was a little irked by the speed with which she had established her distance and he was particularly irked by her statement that there was no way she could become involved with someone like him.

Of course he could understand it. If she happened to be someone on the lookout for a committed relationship. But she wasn't and he believed her. Experiences shaped people and hers had been frightful.

'Because I would be unable to return whatever involvement you wanted?'

Sunny laughed and then looked at him with narrowed, amused, speculative eyes. 'You're really arrogant, aren't you…?'

Stefano frowned, taken aback by her blunt criticism. It was rare for him to meet a woman who wasn't either intimidated by him or else desperate to impress him. With the exception of his mother.

'I don't mean to be offensive,' Sunny hurriedly expanded, 'but there's no way I could ever get involved with someone as rich and powerful and driven as you…'

'Since when are money and ambition turn-offs?' he asked incredulously.

'When I was thirteen,' she mused, looking back into the past, 'I got a scholarship to go to one of the top boarding schools in the country. I met lots of girls there who…came from gilded circles, probably just like you. They talked very loudly in cut-glass accents and laughed a lot and flirted like mad with all the boys. What *they* would have wanted to end up with would have been someone rich and powerful and driven. If I ever find my soulmate, he probably won't have much money and he'll be kind and thoughtful and measured...' *And he'll have to be able to do what you're doing now...he'll have to be able to fire me up until I feel like I can't breathe for the excitement...*

'Forgive me while I stifle a yawn.'

Sunny wanted to be angry at the casual way he had dismissed her heartfelt dreams but when she caught those dark, amused eyes she felt her lips twitch.

'Thoughtful and kind can be very sexy traits.' She lowered her eyes, while the heat of their mutual chemistry sizzled around them.

'Maybe,' Stefano murmured. 'But in the meanwhile...' He tugged her to her feet and she bumped against his hard, muscular body.

She knew this was what it must feel like when swooning women said that they *went up in flames.*

Her whole body was burning, on fire. Her nipples, scraping against her bra, felt insanely sensitive and the dampness between her legs was hot and slick, making her want to reach beneath her underwear so that she could rub herself out of her wet discomfort.

'Yes?' she squeaked, as far removed from the efficient and sexless professional she assumed herself to be as was possible.

'Let me show you what someone raw and elemental can do for you...'

CHAPTER SEVEN

'WHAT ABOUT FLORA?' It sounded like a last-ditch chance to back off and Stefano looked at her with a shuttered expression, as though he could read straight into her mind and pull the thoughts from her head.

'Cold feet?' he asked, without bothering to beat around the bush.

'No!'

'Sure about that?'

'One hundred per cent sure.'

'Even though I'm not the sort of person you should get involved with?'

'This isn't about involvement, is it?' Sunny could scarcely believe she was saying this stuff. She'd done a complete U-turn in the space of a heartbeat. She would never have imagined for a second that lust could be this powerful—powerful enough to bring all her well-laid plans crashing to the ground.

But she was safe emotionally and for that she

was grateful. Her body might be clamouring for adventure but her heart was still switched on enough to know that the real guy for her would not be Stefano Gunn or anyone like him.

'It's just…a one-night stand…' She thought of her fumbling, embarrassing forays into sex, when she had been going out with John. If she'd had the slightest amount of experience she would have known that the missing link had been…*this*. The missing link had been the wild beating of her heart, the aching of her body, the searing excitement at the thought of being touched…

If she'd had the slightest amount of experience, she would have realised that what made perfect sense on paper didn't necessarily translate into perfect sense in practice.

She was here, barely able to breathe for the excitement, and she knew that *this* would have to be part of the equation when she met any man she felt she could have a long-term relationship with.

It wasn't just about personality but it was about *this* as well, without which the personality on its own didn't stand much of a chance.

They were heading up the staircase, softly and quickly, her hand in his. At the top of the staircase, the broad, airy corridor went right for the wing of rooms in which Flora had her bedroom suite and left where Stefano had his rooms.

In her mind's eye, she could picture his huge super-king-size bed and her heart skipped a beat.

She knew that Flora would be sound asleep. Once her head hit the pillow, she slept the deep sleep of a child but on the one occasion when she had had a broken night and Sunny had asked her, the following evening, what she had done, Flora had simply said that she had read until she had fallen asleep again.

His room was in darkness but, instead of switching on the overhead light, he turned on the lamp by the bay window, leaving the curtains open so that weak moonlight filtered into the room.

In the grip of nervous tension, Sunny hovered by the door, which he had quietly shut behind them.

She thought that she might have forgotten how to have sex. Was that possible? A bubble of hysterical laughter threatened...

Looking at her, Stefano could see that she was as nervous as a kitten. She wasn't the sort of girl who moved from one guy to another with seamless ease and he got a disproportionate kick from knowing that she had been unable to resist *him*. It evened the scales because he hadn't been able to resist *her*. Two controlled people *losing it*.

'You're beautiful,' he said softly, beginning to unbutton his shirt, taking his time, exposing his chest sliver by glorious sliver.

Sunny bit back the temptation to tell him that he was as well. That was something he would know, something countless women had probably told him over the years. How could they not? When he was physically...so *perfect*?

She couldn't stop staring. She didn't care that he was looking at her staring at him, a smile tugging the corners of his beautiful mouth.

He shrugged off the shirt and she drank in the broad shoulders, the six-pack stomach, the ripple of muscle, the small flat brown nipples that she itched to tease with her fingers...

Her mouth went dry when he rested his hand on the zip of his trousers. Even from across the room, she could see the unmistakable bulge of his erection, pulsing under the trousers.

'Having fun?' Stefano shot her a wolfish smile that made her toes curl.

Sunny nodded.

'Care to join me in the striptease or would

you rather I took your clothes off for you…? I'm frankly not sure which would turn me on more so…your choice…'

Sunny slipped her fingers under the edge of her stretchy top, feeling as debauched as a stripper in a nightclub, and began slowly tugging it over her breasts and over her head to then toss it onto the ground so that she was now only in her bra and the short controversial skirt.

Stefano walked slowly towards her. There was an innocence in the way she was standing there, hands at her sides, chin at a defiant angle, as though she was fighting against folding her arms across her breasts. And her body was…as spectacular as he had envisaged, long and graceful, with the supple sleekness of a ballet dancer.

His erection was painful, throbbing and pulsing.

'I'm not very experienced at…this sort of thing…' Sunny whispered.

Stefano was now standing directly in front of her and he placed his hands on her shoulders and gently massaged them, relaxing her. 'Me neither…'

Sunny grinned and stole a shy glance at his darkly amused face. But the little teasing joke and the way he was ever so gently massaging her shoulders were doing what they were supposed to do; they were relaxing her. She could feel her whole body thawing out and her breathing slowing.

She sighed softly as she felt him reach behind her to unclasp the bra and her small, high breasts popped out, the rose-pink nipples stiff and pointed.

His low, husky growl of appreciation sent violent ripples of pleasure racing through her.

After a lifetime of playing down her body, it felt incredible to be standing here showing it off and thrilling in his delight.

He cupped them with his big hands and slowly roused both nipples with the pads of his thumbs until she was quivering with excitement, melting, desperate for him to do so much more than just tease.

He was taking his time, slowing his pace. Sunny could *sense* that and she was impressed by the level of thoughtfulness behind that because she could envisage him as a man who was probably accustomed to taking…fast and hard.

He backed her gently against the door and she

stuck her hands behind her, flattened against the door as he began to suckle on her nipples.

Head flung back, eyes closed, Sunny could only whimper with pleasure as his moist mouth relentlessly sucked. Her hands balled into fists behind her back and the whimpers were deepening into moans. When he pulled away she wanted to direct his head right back from whence it had come. Her wet nipples were cooling quickly as he tugged down the skirt, allowing her to wriggle out of it, where it joined the little top on the ground.

Stefano stood up. This leisurely business was taking a lot out of him. He was still wearing his trousers, thank God, because if he had been able to press his erection against her bare skin he felt as if the unthinkable might have happened.

Even the squash of her soft breasts against his chest was teeth-clenchingly difficult to bear.

He cupped her between her legs and felt her wetness. Very slowly, applying just the right amount of pressure, he massaged her down there, watching her face as he did so, enjoying her helpless, heated response. Her nostrils flared and she wriggled against his hand, gyrating her hips.

When he pushed his hand underneath her panties, she drew in a sharp breath and held it as he inserted two fingers, feeling and finding her swollen clitoris and playing with it until she was begging him to stop and then begging him not to stop.

He didn't stop. He kissed her, long and deep, tongues meshing.

'You have to stop…' Sunny gave a half-hearted push against his busy hand '…or I'll…I won't be able to stop myself…'

'Good,' Stefano murmured into her ear, which made her shiver. 'I've always had a soft spot for a woman who just can't stop herself…'

It was so unbearably erotic. The fact that he was half dressed…that his hand was there, pushed underneath her knickers…that his breath in her ear was warm and sexy…that her nipples were rubbing against his chest…

She came with a deep shudder that racked her body and then she fell limply against him and curved her arms around his neck. When her breathing was back to normal, she fell against his neck and nibbled it until he laughed and swung her up to carry her over to the bed in a couple of easy strides.

'Very caveman…' She smiled drowsily, replete

with contentment and already looking forward to touching him and having him touch her again. She feasted greedy eyes on him as he stood by the bed to remove his trousers and boxers. His legs were long and muscular and she took her time appreciating them, took her time letting her eyes drift higher to rest on his impressive, hard-as-steel, erect manhood. The thatch of dark hair in which it nestled was intimidating in its naked virility. Her tummy flipped and she found that she was holding her breath.

'You like that?' Stefano paused to look at her. She was naked. She'd freed herself from her underwear and she was…spectacular. He'd had beautiful women before but she was…unique in a way he couldn't quite put his finger on. There was something intensely alluring about her mixture of intelligence, savvy streetwise toughness and vulnerability.

'If I'm the last sort of guy you would want to be involved with,' he heard himself say in a roughened undertone as he slipped onto the bed next to her, pulling her into him so that their naked bodies were pressed together, 'then I'm guessing that you've never had a caveman before…' He moved against her and she parted her legs.

He nudged his thigh between them and moved it slowly and absently.

Since when did he give a hoot what other men his previous partners had slept with? As far as he was concerned, all of that was an irrelevance.

But he was curious now. Was he the only inappropriate guy she had gone to bed with? Had there been others? She wasn't married, she wasn't engaged and she had no boyfriend so whatever touchy-feely soulmate types she might have encountered clearly hadn't made it past the starting gate.

How come?

Sunny blushed, conscious of her inexperience. 'I haven't,' she said shortly. 'Let's not talk.' She placed a flattened palm on his chest and marvelled at the hardness of his hair-roughened chest. Just the right amount of hair, she thought distractedly, just the right amount to add to that intensely masculine aura.

She wasn't a virgin but she might just as well have been and here she was, with a man with loads of experience and not just experience but experience with some of the most desirable and beautiful women in the world. Sunny wasn't vain but she was honest. Yes, she knew that she had been born with a certain amount of looks, thanks to her gene pool, but she would still be gauche and awkward and she had no inclination to fill him in on her one and only sort of ex-lover. No way.

Why not? Stefano thought irritably, which was such a ridiculous reaction that he almost laughed.

'You're right…there's a time and a place for talking and I've always found that that place isn't in bed…' He licked an erotic trail along her neck while he traced her delicate collarbone with one long brown finger and that finger carried further down to circle a nipple, teasing it with a feathery touch until Sunny could barely lie still in the bed.

She was positively aching for him when his mouth settled at last on one straining, tautened bud, when he pulled it deep into his mouth, licking the tip with his tongue while his other hand played with her other nipple, rolling over it and igniting a blizzard of heated response inside her.

She squirmed, determined that this time she was going to play with him as much as he was playing with her.

She traced the hard lines of his torso and then circled his hard length with her hand. The faint shudder that ran through his body quelled her nerves in a way no amount of soothing chat could ever have done because it proved to her just how much he wanted her. Whatever the length and width and breadth of his experience.

He wanted *her*.

Even though they came from different worlds… even though he could have had any woman on the planet he desired…even though she wasn't posh or sophisticated. He wanted *her*. Right here and right now at this very moment in time.

The strength of their craving was mutual and she could easily lose herself in that knowledge.

Her body took over and seemed to know what to do or maybe, she thought, that was just how it worked when you were really fired up for someone.

Her legs wanted to part and to receive the ministrations of his mouth as he went down on her, licking and teasing and sucking, exploring her in a way that was unimaginable and unimaginably wonderful.

For Stefano, nothing had ever tasted this sweet. When he had begun nuzzling the soft down between her thighs she had automatically, with some embarrassment, protested, tugging at his hair, even though her legs had remained open, welcoming him to explore between them.

Had she never been caressed and kissed there before?

Curiosity had nudged once again past common sense and it had increased as he had felt her heated response to his intimate caresses, had known from the tremble of her slender thighs pressed against his face that she was loving every second of the experience.

Why had no man touched her there before? She'd been strangely shy to start with but there was so much passion there, passion that matched his, and it was like finding a gold mine that just kept on giving.

Had no man roused her to these heights before? It gave him an unholy kick to imagine that he might be the first even though logic told him that the chances of that were frankly non-existent. She was in her twenties and beautiful. She would have had lots of lovers in her past and he wouldn't have been the first to fire her to these heights even though it might feel that he was.

She moved against his mouth and all thoughts vanished from his head as he lost himself in the taste and smell of her, musky…fragrant…perfume to make a man lose his mind…

It was sweet torture to take his time but he did, making sure to explore her and hanging on by a thread as she explored him.

He nudged at her, the blunt head of his penis tantalising her, but that required a level of self-restraint he found he didn't have.

Sunny stilled him. 'I'm not on the Pill.' She was almost at the point of losing control completely. Her body no longer felt like hers. This wasn't the awkward, excruciatingly self-conscious body that had shied away from John's touch, even though she had wanted so badly to be turned on by him. This was another body—a body that seemed to have a will of its own, a body that could melt and go up in flames at the same time. It was a body that excited and amazed and thrilled her.

She dreaded to think that he might pull away from her because she wasn't on any contraception yet why should she be? She'd had no intention of jumping in the sack with anyone any time soon.

'It wouldn't matter if you were.' Stefano reached to the drawer of the bedside cabinet next to the bed and felt for his pack of condoms.

'Wouldn't it?'

'Of course not. Do you honestly think I'd be stupid enough to believe a woman who said that she was on the Pill and couldn't get pregnant?' His lips curled. 'Been there, done that, got the T-shirt. Trust me, you could pop a pill in front of me and I'd still use a condom because if it's one thing I will never again take, it's a chance...'

The depth of his bitterness shocked Sunny and for a split second she saw the man who had locked himself down emotionally, the man who had constructed a fortress of ice around his heart and whilst she knew that none of that should matter a jot to her because she certainly wasn't in it for a relationship, it still was weirdly unsettling. Was this what John had eventually thought when they had both tried their best and come to the conclusion that they had to walk away from one another? That she was locked down emotionally? Frozen where she should have been alive? That she had nothing to give? Not even the generosity of her physical responses?

Stefano sensed just that fleeting second or two when she seemed to disappear, but then she curled her fingers into his hair and arched up to kiss and nibble the side of his mouth, laughing when he pushed her back to kiss her so thoroughly that she wanted to faint.

He was rock-hard as he slipped on the condom in one smooth expert movement, and then he was thrusting in her, loving the warm tightness of her and the motion of her hips as they picked up rhythm, moving under him as though their bodies had been made to do this, to join together in the act of making love.

Sunny clung.

She'd never clung to anyone in her life before. She had learned from an early age that clinging got you nowhere. But she clung now, wishing that she could keep holding him to her for ever, never wanting to let him go and absolutely loving the feel of his lightly perspiring, tightly packed, muscular body under her hands.

Her orgasm was an explosion that took her to another dimension. A slow build, getting faster until she couldn't breathe as he pushed into her, hard, long strokes that drove her wild. She heard someone groaning and realised that it was her.

When they had both finally come back down to earth, with her head resting on his chest, she listened to the steady beat of his heart and the first thing that came to her head was that she didn't want this to be a one-night stand and that was such a scary realisation that she wanted to whimper in panic.

It felt as though someone had pulled a plug she hadn't even known existed and all of a sudden her prized self-control was slipping remorselessly through the plughole.

This wasn't going to do! She'd made love and it felt as though she'd made love for the first time, felt that this was what the fuss was all about, this soaring, wonderful sensation of flying high above the clouds, a feeling of complete and utter union with another human being.

Had that made her vulnerable? Because, if it had, then she was going to have to find a cure pretty damn quick.

She yawned and sat up, slipping her legs over the side of the bed, and he caught her hand and gently tugged her back down.

'Going somewhere?'

Sunny flipped her long hair to one side and glanced at him over her shoulder. 'To get dressed.'

'Why are you going to do that?' He stroked the underside of her wrist lazily.

'Because it's after midnight and I need to get home.'

'You don't need to get home. There are too many bedrooms in this house to count. You can have your pick.'

Sunny noted that he hadn't suggested she share his room with him but he wouldn't, would he? He knew the lines that had to be drawn. Where she suspected she still had the capacity to melt, he was as hard as steel.

'If Eric can't drive me to the station, I can call a taxi.'

Stefano sat up and frowned. 'You don't want to do that...' He tugged her a little bit more so that she fell back against the pillow and he cupped one breast with his hand, teasing the nipple into a stiff, throbbing peak. 'And your nipple agrees with me...'

Sunny wriggled. Of course, this was his great strength, she thought. It wasn't his looks, incredible though they were, or his bank balance or the house he lived in or the helicopter he owned or the cars he drove... It was his searing intelligence and his wicked sense of humour. Both those things could be her undoing.

She smacked his hand and he laughed and caught it and then twisted her to face him so that he could nibble the tips of her fingers one by one.

'I'd bet there are other parts of your body,' he continued in that same devastatingly sexy, low voice, 'that would also be in agreement... Shall we discover which bits?'

'Stefano, this was just meant to be a one-night stand...' But she heard the weakness in her voice with alarm. She sounded as though she was trying to convince herself of what she was saying and she knew that he would be able to see straight through her half-hearted protest.

Her body was responding to his casual touch. She thought, in retrospect, that she should have leaped off the bed in one athletic bound and shoved on her clothes before he had time to reach out and touch her. The second he'd touched her, all her good intentions seemed to have gone up in smoke.

'The road to Hell...' He left the quote unfinished and she made a valiant effort to listen to her head and remove her treacherous body from the equation. 'Don't you want to carry on this process of discovery for longer than just a few hours?' He lowered his dark head to take the same nipple he had been caressing into his mouth and he sucked on it very slowly and very, very erotically, half looking at her so that their eyes were tangling as he continued to nip and suck and flick his tongue over her nipple.

He levered himself up to look down at her seriously and Sunny hated knowing that she just wanted him to return to what he was doing, turning her on.

'It's not a good idea,' she mumbled.

'We're both adults…we both fancy one another…where's the problem?'

'I…I'm not looking for any kind of complicated situation…' Her voice petered out and she worried her lip anxiously.

'Snap.' Stefano pressed her back against the bed, pinning her arms on either side and raking his eyes over her stunning breasts. 'Nor am I…'

'I barely know you…' Sunny felt as though she was running round in circles. Her objections made no sense. He didn't want a relationship and neither did she…and yes, they fancied one another. But surely there should be *something more* than that if they were to continue sleeping with one another?

'You know more about me than anyone else,' he murmured, sifting his long fingers through her hair.

And that was true, he thought with a certain

amount of surprise. She knew his motivations, knew his circumstances...*knew his daughter.* And he certainly knew a fair amount about her, or he fancied he did because she was a private person. That was something he *felt* and something he rather *liked.*

'How well do you think you have to know someone in a case like this?' Stefano mused. 'Neither of us predicted that this would happen and yet here we are. It did. Somehow we bypassed all the usual verbal foreplay and ended up in bed because we frankly can't resist one another...but we both share the same pragmatic take on what we have...'

Sunny wasn't sure that *pragmatic* was such a thrilling way to describe what was happening. 'Meaning?'

'We both know that this isn't going to last but we're happy to enjoy it while it does. Neither of us is interested in anything...*complicated*... We're going into it with our eyes wide open and that works for me and I imagine it works for you as well...'

'I just never thought that I'd...be the sort of person to jump into bed with a guy I barely know simply for the sake of sex.'

'Scintillating, mind-blowing sex…'

'You're very egotistic.' But she laughed softly and helplessly.

'It takes two to contribute to scintillating, mind-blowing sex…and, since you're without a boyfriend, I'm guessing that you might have jumped into bed with guys you knew well and yet…ended up in relationships that weren't going anywhere. Am I right?'

'You're so black and white.'

'You see clearer when things are black and white.' He circled her nipple with his finger and then gently flicked a teasing tongue over the tip, before returning his gaze to her face. 'Too much grey has a nasty habit of blurring the lines. And sometimes it pays not to overthink a situation… but just to lie back and enjoy it…'

'Good job!'

Flora was clapping by the side of the pool. In the shade, Stefano was lying on a lounger, having abandoned the effort of reading the money section of the Sunday broadsheet.

He had tamed his uneasy conscience.

In front of Flora, he and Sunny were simply two adults who communicated and did the occasional joint thing with her, Flora, as the central focus. Flora was basking in it and opening up more and more daily. How could that be a bad thing? In due course, he and Sunny would fizzle out and she would disappear. Of course, should his daughter wish to continue to communicate, there was always email. He would never stop that. As for him…whilst he knew the day they went their separate ways was inevitable, he would enjoy it while it lasted.

The sex was mind-blowing. What was there to worry about? He felt as if he'd recaptured all the self-control he had momentarily lost before they had become lovers.

Sunny was proudly clinging to the side of the pool, having completed her first lap underwater.

Looking down at that summer scene, anyone might have been forgiven for thinking that this was picture-perfect domesticity. Sunny knew better than to allow herself to wallow in such illusions. She and Stefano were now *an item*. An *item* that had been going on for three weeks—an *item* that Flora seemed to accept with the casualness of an eight-year-old, not that Sunny quite knew *what* Flora thought of the situation.

Certainly, Sunny and Stefano *never* exchanged

any physical shows of affection in front of his daughter. But, on the other hand, Sunny was at the house a lot. Most evenings, even though there was no longer any need for her to be there and even though she had refused all payment, knowing that it would make her feel cheap should she take money from him while sleeping with him.

'Don't be ridiculous,' Stefano had told her. 'You're here looking after Flora before I return home…you need to differentiate between business and pleasure. Babysitting my daughter is business, for which you deserve payment.'

'If you pay me anything,' Sunny had told him, 'then I'll walk away and never come back.'

Although how easy would that have been? Like an addict, she couldn't seem to control herself when she was around him and when she wasn't around him she was thinking of him. In the space of a heartbeat, she had gone from focusing one hundred per cent on her job to focusing on Stefano.

His face popped up when she was gazing at her computer screen. His voice rang in her head when she was in the office canteen having lunch with the other employees. His smile appeared when she was staring down at columns of legal precedents and then she had to blink for it to disappear.

When Flora was around, they had meals together. Gradually, Sunny could see Flora warming to her father, interacting with him before retreating behind the surliness she had mastered over the months, although now that surliness was half-hearted, the remnants of a habit that was gradually being whittled away, not least because her father was around a lot more than he had ever been.

He hadn't missed the small changes in his daughter and he was generous in laying the reward for that at her door.

'That's down to you,' Stefano had told her two nights before and Sunny's heart had melted at the uneven roughness of his voice, which he had not been able to conceal. 'Let me pay you. I want to. You have done far more than words can say.'

Sunny had refused. Indeed, she could even have said that, for everything she had done for Flora, Flora had done a great deal for *her*. She had sat and played games on the computer. One afternoon, when Stefano had brought her down to London, they had gone shopping and Sunny had been exposed to a vision of all the clothes an eight-year-old could buy and what a shopping trip might have been like had she had a mother to go on one with. They had, the weekend before, gone to the zoo in Regent's Park so that Flora could see that not all zoos were unethical. It was somewhere Sunny had never visited. She had been enthralled and captivated. There had been a child's party there, a chattering and excitable group of a dozen kids. Was that what normality would have felt like? She'd closed her eyes and tried it on for size in her head. She'd pictured how normality would have felt if she'd been Flora's age.

And this...being by the pool with Flora and Stefano...*felt normal* and that scared her because she knew that it shouldn't.

She just didn't understand what was happening to her. Stefano made no more sense now than he had on day one. He was still utterly inappropriate. Was she just maturing late? Was this the equivalent of a sixteen-year-old's crush? This racing heart, sweaty palms, sweetly aching...*thing*?

Had she made the big mistake of trying to figure everything out, trying to make sure that everything, including emotions, had their rightful place on a spreadsheet...and in the process not allowed for the power of impulse?

If that were the case, then it would be a relief to get this out of her system. What if she had married? Settled down? Only for someone like Stefano to blaze into her life out of nowhere, railroading everything in its path, including her well-thought-out life plan? How much worse would it have been if this sort of reckless craziness had happened later on down the road!

She leaned at the side of the pool and watched him, stretched out on the lounger, all packed muscle and virile masculine appeal.

She'd stayed the night before but always in a separate room. And before she tiptoed her way there…the memory of their bodies locked together as one could still make her feel a little giddy.

Now, she felt that familiar heat course through her body at what lay ahead. His touch, his mouth, the feel of him…were embedded in her like a burr under her skin, something always there, reminding her of his presence in her life.

Flora was giving her a series of further swimming instructions which included such gems as, 'Try not to breathe underwater!' and, 'Don't sink to the bottom!' or, 'Remember to think like a fish!'

Diving down and holding her breath, Sunny wondered what any self-respecting fish would think if it found itself in a massive turquoise swimming pool in the middle of an English commuter-belt village. Probably die of shock and... drown.

She was smiling, perfectly content, when she surfaced on the other side of the pool to shake water out of her hair, turning around automatically, the way her body seemed to do whenever Stefano was in the vicinity, seeking him out like a heat-guided missile seeking out a source of warmth...

Hair everywhere, water dripping down her face, rubbing her eyes as she levered herself out of the pool, she was expecting nothing more than Flora, who would probably be clapping as though she had invented the art of teaching another person how to swim, and Stefano, who would be looking at them both with that dry amusement that made her want to reach out and touch him.

Instead...

A small dark-haired woman was standing next to Stefano, staring at the pool, mouth open as though the pause button had been pressed at the very moment she had been about to say something.

In fact…when she looked at Stefano…

He looked a little grey round the gills. He looked as though he would quite have liked to have been able to press the delete button…

Only Flora seemed oblivious and Sunny gratefully settled her eyes on her whilst simultaneously wondering…

What the heck's going on?

CHAPTER EIGHT

FEELING AS CONSPICUOUS as a rattlesnake at a tea party, Sunny stood awkwardly at the side of the pool in the ubiquitous black bikini. Never had she felt so underdressed. The woman gaping at her, in her midsixties, was impeccably dressed and impeccably groomed. Although the temperature was in the seventies, she was in a neat skirt and a blouse with a bow at the neck and a jacket that matched the pale yellow skirt. And the shoes, likewise, matched the rest of the outfit.

'Stefano?' The older woman turned to him and Sunny took advantage to dash for her towel, which she secured around her body, and then she remained where she was, not knowing whether she should introduce herself or pretend that she wasn't really there at all.

Because she had worked out who this must be. Stefano's mother.

'She's just back from Scotland,' he had casually dropped into the conversation a couple of evenings before, 'but you needn't fear that she'll unexpectedly turn up. My mother is extremely traditional in most things and that includes what she sees as the annoying habit some people have of showing up unannounced. Appointments should be made so that tea can be prepared.'

'Even with you?' Sunny had laughed, thinking yet again how wildly different their worlds were.

'Even with me,' he had confirmed wryly. 'If I were to show up on her doorstep she would immediately think that something was wrong.'

'And what about Flora? What if Flora were to show up on her doorstep?'

'She'd be beside herself with joy,' Stefano had admitted honestly. 'Flora has been…difficult with me but only slightly better with my mother. I'm very much hoping things might change on that front… Tea's planned for next weekend.'

And that was a family gathering from which she would be excluded. Sunny knew that and expected nothing different, but it had still hurt somewhere deep inside her.

Nerves gripped her as a pair of dark eyes, very much like Stefano's, once more returned to look at her with eagle-eyed curiosity and interest.

Flora had bounded out of the water and was

busily inspecting a tartan skirt that had been brought back for her.

'It'll look great with those black shoes of yours,' Sunny said, if only to break the silence.

'It seems my son hasn't been as forthcoming as he might have been!'

'Mother, this is...'

'I'm Sunny—' she stretched out her hand, determined to set things straight and save both herself and Stefano the awkward embarrassment of trying to sweep her under the carpet '—and I look after Flora now and again. When your son has to work late.'

'For example—' the sharp black eyes were twinkling with humour '—on a weekend? Stefano?' She turned to her son and fixed him with a beady stare. 'What are you working on, lying on a sun lounger by the side of the pool? A tan? Because I don't seem to see that cursed laptop computer of yours anywhere!' She turned back to Sunny. 'Not that I'm not overjoyed to find him without that thing attached to his arm! I am! Now, why don't we all go inside for a nice cup of tea? Here for a reason, Stefano! Quite slipped my mind with all the excitement of finding you out here with a nice young lady you never saw fit to tell your old mother about!' She began striding back towards the house, but not until she had carolled over her shoulder, 'This is not the way I raised my son! I thought…I *thought* I'd raised a respectful young man who would have been the first to tell me that he was in a serious relationship!'

Aghast, Sunny looked around to see whether Flora had heard this telling throwaway remark and, thankfully, she was still too busy burrowing into the package on the poolside table to pay them much notice.

Serious relationship? How much further from the truth could his mother get?

She excused herself as soon as she was inside, mumbling and stuttering something about getting changed. Stefano was as comfortable in his dry swimming trunks and a T-shirt as if he had been dressed in a suit but she, on the other hand, was burning up with mortification.

Flora had scampered upstairs to try on the bundle of clothes and look at the artists' materials that had been presented to her, beautifully wrapped and, Sunny could immediately see, chosen with love and care.

'Coming back down?' Sunny peeped into the

room to see her absorbed in one of the colouring books with felt pens neatly laid out on the desk in front of her. 'Your…er…grandmother would be overjoyed to…um…chat with you…'

'Think I'll stay here for a bit,' Flora said chirpily then her smile faded and she chewed her lips thoughtfully. 'It was nice of Nana to bring this stuff back, I guess.'

'Very nice.'

'She says she's got loads of other stuff at her house that she hasn't got round to showing me…'

'She seems very kind,' Sunny said gently and Flora flushed. 'And you must never worry that you may have offended her if you were a bit confused and quiet when you first came over here,' she continued, 'because she also seems a wise old bird and she'll have understood that everything in life takes time…including getting to know someone… You can't rush stuff like that…'

'I've agreed to go spend the night there.' Flora returned to her colouring. 'So I'll be down in a little while. I'm just going to do a bit more of this and then I'm going to pack a bag.'

Which meant that Sunny was heading back down the stairs without the bolstering support of her little charge. She had no idea what to expect or even where she might find Stefano and his mother but she headed first for the kitchen and, sure enough, there they were. His mother was sitting upright in a chair, with a cup of tea next to her and a little dish of biscuits, while Stefano stood by the French windows, back to the sprawling lawns, the very picture of discomfort.

'My son has not even chosen to introduce us properly,' were her opening words as she briskly stood up, hand outstretched, as though they were being introduced for the first time. 'I am Angela and I know your name is Sunny, but why don't you sit and tell me a bit about yourself?' She shot Stefano a disapproving look. 'Although,' she added, 'I can see for myself that you have had a tremendous influence on the household.' She smiled and Sunny smiled back because under the stern exterior she could sense a genuine innate warmth.

'I...' She looked at Stefano for help and he shot her a rueful, wry smile.

'Stefano tells me that you two have been seeing each other for a little while...'

'He has?' Sunny squeaked, not sure whether to be pleased that he had not tried to erase her out of his life because of her lack of suitability or confused because he hadn't.

'Of course I understand now why he didn't mention you to me...'

'You do?' Sunny sidled over to a chair and sat down because her legs felt like jelly.

'He wanted to be sure...'

'Sure of what?' Sunny asked faintly.

'Sure that you weren't going to be another of those two-week affairs he seems to enjoy having!' She sipped some of her tea and stared thoughtfully at Sunny over the rim of the delicate china cup which he had managed to unearth from somewhere. 'Of course, there was no need for him to tell me that,' she said comfortably. 'I knew the very moment I saw you with Flora...'

'Ah...'

'But we can talk about all this later. For the moment...well...' She turned to Stefano. She was so small and he was so impossibly tall that she had to stare up and up to meet his eyes. 'You will simply have to see about this situation, Stefano. I can't bear the thought of anything precious being ruined and I'm very much afraid that if it's not sorted immediately, that's exactly what will happen. Now, my dear girl—' she patted Sunny on the shoulder and offered another of those wonderfully warm smiles that could melt ice '—I very much look forward to really getting to know you but, for the moment, I'm going to have to hurry off. I only dropped by because this was something of an emergency. My son knows that I absolutely loathe turning up on someone's doorstep when they might be in the middle of doing something and simply can't spare the time…and Flora has agreed to come with me. I can't tell you how overjoyed I am at that. I'll go and fetch her…'

'I'll get her.'

But Angela overruled her son and was already leaving the kitchen, calling behind her that she wanted to see what Flora had in her room so that she could know what sorts of presents to get for her.

'I can't wait to be a proper grandmother,' she said wistfully. 'I never thought the day would come when Flora would actually want to spend time with me. I'll show myself out, Stefano, but I expect you to get back to me about this problem with the house!'

She disappeared, leaving behind her the sort of flat anti-climax that followed a particularly impressive natural event.

Stefano looked at Sunny carefully and cursed himself for the awkward situation in which he now found himself.

Sunny had the stunned look of someone who had been thrown a blinder when they were least expecting it.

'My mother occasionally has that effect on people,' he drawled, leaning on the table, hands gripping the edge. 'She says that's how she managed to get my father. She blew into his life like a whirlwind and, before he knew what was going on, they were blissfully wed. I'm going to change and make sure my mother gets off okay with Flora. I don't want my daughter to suddenly change her mind about going. I'll be back down in ten.'

'Why did she think that we're involved in some kind of *serious relationship*?' was the first thing Sunny asked when, fifteen minutes later, he strolled into the kitchen in a pair of chinos and a white polo shirt.

She'd had a little time to think and it made no sense. He had given her enough cautionary tales about his lack of interest in commitment. He had warned her that he didn't do relationships of any kind. *Once bitten, twice shy* had been his resounding motto since they had started sleeping together.

So why would he have left his mother with the impression that this was something more than it really was? If anything, he should have been keen to make it clear to her that it was nothing of the sort!

'My mother's relationship with Flora, as I may have mentioned to you, has been…fragile. When my ex-wife disappeared to the other side of the world with our daughter, she made it nigh on impossible for me to keep in touch with her and flouted every custody law that had been set in stone as much as she possibly could. As a result, I had very little contact with Flora over the years. Naturally, I employed lawyers to try and remedy the situation but a mother has strong rights to retain custody of children and I had next to no grounds for removing custody from her hands. I was travelling a great deal, rarely in the country for longer than a couple of weeks at a time. Alicia was fully aware of that and used it to her advantage.'

'That must have been awful for you.' She thought that it was heartbreaking for a parent to be denied the opportunity to see his own child. Didn't she know, first-hand, how desperately a child craved the attention of his or her parent?

When she'd accepted this temporary job to babysit Flora, getting past her initial reluctance because the job paid well, little had she known that she would end up engaging like this in their family drama. But then again, she wasn't to know that she would end up sleeping with the guy who had employed her, was she? Against all possible odds. And how could she have guessed that she would have become attached to Flora when she'd never seen herself as particularly interested in children at all?

'Hence the reason why my relationship with my daughter has been understandably strained. The same can be said for my mother, who had even less contact with Flora over the years. Indeed, practically none at all after she was removed to New Zealand.'

'I'm sorry to hear that.'

'She tried hard,' Stefano said, 'and hasn't stopped. Of course, Flora was less…surly with my mother than she has been with me, but there hasn't been any gush of warmth, which my mother has been craving.'

'I guess these things will always take time…
er…considering what Flora's been through…'

'And there you have it,' Stefano said in the tri-
umphant voice of a head teacher praising his
prized pupil for getting the answer right.

'There you have what?' Sunny was confused.

'The marvel of the breakthrough,' he elaborated with a broad sweep of his hands, a gesture
that mesmerised her so that she had to blink herself back to what they were discussing. 'Flora has
changed. I have noticed this but the change has
not just been with me. It seems that her attitude
is changing…that she's beginning to accept that
I'm not an evil monster, that this house isn't a
loathsome prison, that my mother isn't a wicked
witch trying to tempt her with candy canes…
and you have been instrumental in this change.'

Sunny flushed with pleasure but hastened to
downplay the compliment.

'No!' Stefano halted her in midflow with one
raised hand. 'Don't try to deny it! It's the truth.'
He tilted his head to one side and looked at her
consideringly. 'Before I go any further, you're
probably wondering why my mother showed up
when I mentioned to you in the past that she's

the last person in the world for such displays of spontaneity…'

It dimly occurred to Sunny that they had strayed from the beaten track and her original shock that his mother had misconstrued what was going on, but she nodded in a trance-like way, with the weird feeling of being swept away on a sudden, unexpected and very powerful rip-tide over which she seemed to have no control.

'There's been a problem with my mother's house in Scotland…'

'I thought your mother lived in London…'

'She does but she hangs onto the family home up there. Sentimental reasons. It's where she and my father lived before he died. She still has many friends there and goes up frequently to visit them.' He waved aside that digression. 'But the house is old and prone to the usual aches and pains of any old property. It seems that there's been something of a flood and certain…possessions have had to be salvaged and moved to another part of the house. At any rate, my mother is now panicked at the thought that things she treasures will be destroyed should the huge leak not be fixed to the right standard.' He shrugged his broad shoulders and relaxed back in the chair.

'She's called on me to take a week off so that I can go up there with her and Flora, of course, to assess the damage and make the workmen know that there's a deadline on doing the job.'

Searing disappointment tore through her but she maintained a bright smile.

This was a 'Dear John' speech. He was off to Scotland and would diplomatically get rid of her before he went so that he could disabuse his mother of whatever misconceptions she was labouring under.

She'd known from the start that longevity wasn't going to be part of what they had—hadn't *wanted* longevity—but she was still…disappointed.

'When do you leave?' she asked politely and Stefano shot her a guarded smile.

'If my mother declares that she wants me to do something, she wants me to do it the day before yesterday. I'll leave first thing tomorrow morning.'

'Of course.' There was an awkward little silence during which Sunny tried to work out how she was going to say what had to be said. 'I'll say goodbye to Flora before I leave and perhaps

I could visit her now and again during the holidays? Naturally, when you're not around...'

'What are you talking about?'

'Us...' she said a little tersely, although the smile remained fixed in place. 'This...I do realise that your mother got hold of the wrong end of the stick and you plan on telling her the truth when you have her on your own...'

'And your response to that is to tell me that you're off but you'll visit Flora now and again when I'm not around?'

'You don't have to worry,' Sunny told him stiffly, 'that I'm going to make a nuisance of myself by trying to prolong whatever it is that we have going on between us.'

'I admit my mother was surprised to find...what must have appeared a cosy domestic scene...'

'You should have told her the truth. I felt very awkward at having to act as though this is a proper relationship. I don't believe in lying to people.'

'My mother,' Stefano said bluntly, 'is clearly aware that you have been instrumental in Flora's change of attitude. The last time she and Flora spoke, Flora was, as usual, stiff and unforthcoming. Now, of her own volition, she will be spending the night with my mother…' He allowed a small pause, during which he wondered about the ramifications of what he was on the brink of doing. For every action wasn't there always a *re*-action? In other words, *a consequence*?

Sunny didn't say anything. They seemed to be going round in circles, even though she had the uneasy feeling that Stefano's circles made complete sense to him, whilst leaving her totally in the dark.

'This is something she has no desire to jeopardise…'

'I understand that.' Sunny's green eyes were sympathetic although she had no idea what any of this had to do with her.

'And to return to your original question…'

'Yes…about your mother jumping to conclusions…'

'It's not entirely incomprehensible. I've never asked any woman to this house before…'

'You haven't?'

'I tend to keep my private life alive and kicking in London…'

Sunny was beginning to get wild ideas that he had seen something special in her when she remembered, before any stupid wild ideas could take root, that she hadn't come here in the capacity of his girlfriend. She had come here as Flora's babysitter and only after she was here had the whole girlfriend angle come into play.

'And I certainly have never introduced any woman to Flora.'

'Yes, but it was different with me,' Sunny pointed out reasonably. 'I was here *because* of Flora...'

'No matter.' He shrugged while keeping his eyes fixed on her face. 'The scene that presented itself to my mother was not one of the nanny looking after her charge. The three of us were by the pool, which, in my case, is virtually unheard of. Flora was laughing and relaxed, as were you.'

'I can understand that...'

'We're lovers, Sunny,' Stefano interrupted abruptly. 'The order of events might not be quite in line with my mother's conclusions but we're still involved with one another and Flora is part of that equation...'

'So what are you saying?'

'My mother may not have approved of the women I've gone out with but she has trusted me never to allow any of them to overstep the boundaries. In other words, they've been kept in London. She assumes that this relationship is rather more serious because those boundary lines have been overstepped. She's also seeing what she has desperately wanted to see for a while, namely a contender for the role of surrogate mother to Flora and much needed wife for me... Naturally, as we both know, that's not on the agenda...'

'Absolutely not!' Sunny looked appropriately horrified. She thought that his mother might have had a lot more reservations if she knew just how unsuitable she was for her son.

'However...'

'However?' Sunny prompted when he failed to continue and Stefano shot her a speculative look from under his long dark lashes.

'Like I said, the situation, she feels, between herself and her granddaughter is...fragile. And, with a week in Scotland looming, she doesn't want to lose those little gains that have been made...and she feels that the only way that can be assured is if you come.'

It took a few seconds for Sunny to digest what he was saying and then she blinked at him, wondering whether she had misheard what he'd said.

'If *I* come?' Sunny laughed uncertainly. 'I can't come with you to Scotland!'

Stefano banked down a spurt of irritation. This was her way of reminding him that the situation between them was transient and involved nothing beyond having fun in bed. He couldn't stop the flare of his libido when he thought about *just how much fun.*

This was *exactly* the sort of response that should have made his day. A sexy, responsive woman who knew the parameters of what they had and was comfortable with them…a woman who was on precisely the same wavelength as he was. He'd had more than his fair share over the years of women who had ended up wanting more than he was capable of giving and to be with one like Sunny should have heralded the sort of blessed relief that a breeze brought on a stiflingly hot day.

He was annoyed with himself to discover that the blessed breezy relief was absent.

She hadn't even toyed with the thought of coming with him! Hadn't even given it house room! Shouldn't she be *thrilled to death* that he'd asked her? 'If it's about taking time off work, then I'm sure that wouldn't be a problem,' he gritted. 'Even the most dedicated and ambitious of staff need to take time off now and again…'

'It's not about taking time off work,' Sunny said jerkily.

What was it about? Really?

She knew what. It was about the dangers of sinking further and faster into this little family unit that didn't belong to her and never would. She'd never anticipated any of this and she felt as though she'd been taken over, as though her days were now spent in anticipation of the evenings and being with Stefano and Flora. Having spent a lifetime on the outside of family units like this, it scared her just how much she enjoyed being inside one—inside this one. This wasn't her family unit and she was just a stranger peering in through the open door.

The thought of going to Scotland, of getting to know his mother, would be just another dangerous and seductive step closer to finding all of this...indispensable. It was a terrifying prospect because nothing in life should ever be indispensable.

'Then what is it about?' Stefano asked, his voice cooler.

'I don't think it's a good idea if I get any more involved...I mean, this was just supposed to be a one-night stand...wasn't it? Also, it's not fair to your mother, is it? I mean, if she thinks that this is something it isn't...'

'I understand your reservations.' Stefano's voice was more clipped than he had intended and he raked his fingers through his hair. 'Of course, it would be preferable if she wasn't labouring under the illusion that this is anything significant, but there's more at stake here than my mother getting the wrong end of the stick.'

Labouring under the illusion that this is anything significant... Those words got stuck in Sunny's brain and played round and round on a loop. She was *insignificant*. Whichever way you looked at it, that was the upshot. *She was insignificant and didn't mean anything at all outside good sex and a bit of fun.*

'Sorry?' She surfaced to find that she had missed what he'd been saying.

'I can't force you to come to Scotland,' Stefano said heavily. 'If the anticipated one-night stand is in danger of outstaying its welcome, then by all means I will tell my mother that it's over, that it was never anything serious anyway...'

'And it isn't.' Sunny was trying to get her head around the prospect of never seeing Stefano again.

'But if I tell her that this is over, then it's over.

No visits to my daughter and no second thoughts. Even when I acknowledged my attraction to you, I was reluctant to act on it because I didn't want to risk a setback in my new-found relationship with Flora. We break up and you disappear, because having you knocking around now and again will only muddy the waters. I can't stop you emailing but that would have to be the size of it. Ready for that?'

And he wouldn't have a problem with that. There hadn't been a hitch in his voice when he had flatly stated that fact. He didn't want it to end just yet but he was a pragmatist first and foremost. If it ended, it ended.

'This is the first time Flora has agreed to do anything with my mother since she came to this country and my mother is anxious that she doesn't pull away when they're in Scotland. Children don't tend to think rationally and they don't look at the bigger picture or necessarily see the consequences of their actions. Your presence, I think, would be of great help...but I can't force you.'

Sunny was feverishly thinking over the gauntlet he had thrown down. Was she ready to go cold turkey? Was she ready to walk away and never look back? 'But surely your mother will find out sooner or later, when this is all over, that it was never serious...'

'Every day, with any luck, her relationship with Flora will strengthen...'

'So she won't really care if I'm no longer around because she will have the sort of relationship she wants with her granddaughter. And I guess, when she finds out the sort of person I am, she'll be mightily relieved that you're no longer involved with me...'

'The *sort of person*?'

'The sort that comes from the wrong side of the tracks.' She hated herself for even mentioning something as silly as that. She had always been determined that she would not carry a chip on her shoulder because of her background. It was true that she kept herself to herself, but that was force of habit, instilled from an early age. Her past had shaped her and for that she would always be grateful.

So why on earth insinuate that she would be seen as not good enough for him?

And why the heck did it matter anyway?

'You're assuming that my mother is a snob,' Stefano said coolly.

'I shouldn't have said that. It honestly doesn't matter anyway,' she tacked on. She took a deep breath and looked him squarely in the face. 'I'll see if I can take the week off work and if I can, then fine, I'll come.'

Stefano only knew that he had been tense when he felt himself relax. Of course, he dismissed, he would be tense. The sudden appearance of his mother and the conclusions she had mistakenly jumped to had altered events and, much as he didn't like the fact that she thought that he and Sunny were in some sort of *serious relationship*, he liked even less thinking that she would be fearful and nervous about Flora being in Scotland and apprehensive in case his daughter did an about-turn and decided to retreat back into the shell from which she had only so very recently emerged.

He recognised that he wasn't ready to say goodbye to the frankly stupendous sex they shared, but that, he firmly told himself, was not a cause for tension. Had she decided that she couldn't go through with the minor pretence for the sake of his mother, then letting her go would have been regrettable but no more difficult than with any of the women he had slept with in the past.

'Are your reasons purely altruistic?' he murmured, with a slow, lazy smile that made her toes curl and brought hectic colour to her cheeks. He hadn't meant to ask that and he grudgingly acknowledged that the question, at least in part, stemmed from the fact that he had been disconcerted and taken aback by the ease with which she appeared to have thought about dumping what they had.

He almost laughed at the notion of a man like him requiring reassurance!

'Of course they are!' But she smiled and dipped her eyes, breath catching in her throat as he stood up to pull his chair closer to hers so that their knees were touching.

There were times when just the hot burn of his eyes on her was enough to make her wet for him, was almost enough to start the slow tremor of an orgasm.

This was one of those times.

'So...are you telling me that I don't figure in your decision-making process at all? Because a man could be hurt...'

'Maybe you do figure...a tiny bit...'

'I feel I shall have to show you just how much I actually do figure... We have the house all to ourselves… We could continue the swimming lessons but without the annoying encumbrance of a swimsuit.'

It sounded wildly decadent. Oddly, for someone whose life had been disjointed and challenging, Sunny was not wild or decadent. Her mother had been a steep learning curve in *how not to be*. Short skirts and small clothes and random men… never mind the drugs and the drink… Sunny had rebelled by being the complete opposite. Restraint, self-control and background clothes had been her way of keeping shut the lid of Pandora's box. If she cracked at all, who knew what might happen? She was, after all, her mother's daughter. That, she thought, had been the way her subconscious had worked, which just went to disprove Stefano's theory that black and white was the safest vision to choose. Because she was living in the grey area now and loving it. Swimming naked in a pool wasn't going to turn her into her mother. Swimming naked in a pool was just going to be *fun* and she could see that in closing herself off from anything that could remotely be interpreted as *unsafe* she had also closed herself off from all sorts of experiences that were enjoyable.

She laughed, her bright green eyes gleaming as they met his.

'I've never done anything like that in my life before,' she confided, allowing him to pull her to her feet and then falling against him and staying there, arms around his waist as she stared up at his dangerously handsome face. 'I've always played it safe…'

'Skinny-dipping isn't anything outrageous,' Stefano told her drily, liking the bone-deep sincerity in everything she said and did, the absolute lack of artifice.

'You'd be surprised how outrageous it is for me.' Sunny laughed and he bent his head to kiss the side of her mouth, then covered her mouth with his, deepening the kiss until she was squirming in his embrace.

He could have taken her right here, right now. His erection was rock-hard and he figured that a dip in the pool might take care of that little problem, at least temporarily. Because he wanted to enjoy her at his leisure.

'It turns me on to know that I'm the guy who's going to take you places you've never been,' he confessed in a driven murmur.

And when the trip's over, you'll return to where

you belong and...where will that leave me? The sudden prospect of him disappearing out of her life as suddenly as he had entered it gave her a sickening, swooping feeling in the pit of her stomach. She didn't know what it meant and she didn't want to analyse it, but she did know that it was something unwelcome and something he should not suspect. Instinct told her that.

'And I'm glad you are.' Sunny sighed, angling her body so that he could work his hand over her flat stomach to caress between her legs, cupping her over her underwear and rubbing his finger so that the cotton of her briefs pushed into her wetness. 'I mean...I was innocent before I met you...'

'And now?'

'I feel like I've...joined the human race. I feel like I've learned that taking chances isn't always a bad thing and won't always lead to rack and ruin.' She laughed and reached up to kiss him, pulling him into her and pressing hard against him.

'So you're now going to be wild and reckless...' Stefano wasn't sure why he found that concept so deeply unappealing.

'Not wild and reckless,' Sunny said honestly,

'but maybe less careful. I mean…if it can feel this good with you, how will it feel when I'm with my for ever guy…?'

It would be brilliant. Since John, she had resigned herself to the life of being a career woman and had not been unhappy with her decision, but everything had changed. Stefano had unlocked the passionate, responsive woman in her, the woman who could bring the full package to any relationship she would go on to have, any relationship with a guy who would be her soulmate.

Of course it made sense that if she could feel this good with Stefano, who was just passing through her life, then it would be beyond good with the man who would be staying for keeps. She tried to imagine what this guy might look like and the dark, sexy image of Stefano's face swam into focus and stayed there.

Stefano thought that there was such a thing as *too much honesty*. Was it really on to talk about his successor even though their relationship was still ongoing? He felt the sharp jab of undiluted *jealousy* towards this non-existent fictional character who had yet to appear on the scene.

It was laughable.

Except he found that he wasn't laughing.

'Who knows?' he asked in a rough, husky undertone. 'Maybe you'll find that it just won't be as good…' And if the challenge, stupid though it was, was to prove that to her, to take her to heights she couldn't conceivably reach with anyone else, then who was he to back down from the challenge?

CHAPTER NINE

BEING IN SCOTLAND showed Sunny just how much she had forgotten about the art of pure relaxation.

She'd been apprehensive about the trip. Even when, the day after she had agreed to go, she found herself climbing into the helicopter that would make short work of the trip to Perthshire, she was still questioning the wisdom of sinking even deeper into Stefano and his family.

She'd almost half hoped that she would be told that the company couldn't spare her, but in fact she had talked to Katherine, who had been delighted that she was having some time off.

'Going anywhere nice?' she had asked and Sunny had guiltily been as creative with the truth as she could be without resorting to any outright lies.

Stefano might have said that he wasn't interested in Katherine, but was Katherine interested in *him*? She couldn't see how the other woman could fail to be and she had no desire to step on any toes or instigate any bad feeling between them which would follow her through her career at the company.

Especially when you considered that whatever she and Stefano had, permanence wasn't part of the equation.

She could also understand why his mother might feel apprehensive about the fragile seedlings of the relationship she was building with her granddaughter. Flora had arrived in a new family, full of resentment and dislike, and Angela Gunn was cautious about believing that there had been a turnaround that wouldn't disappear as fast as it had surfaced.

And anyway, she had thought with a spurt of reckless abandon, sleeping with Stefano was the first thing she had ever done on wild impulse and why shouldn't she enjoy it while she could? She'd already thrown caution to the winds when she had climbed into bed with him, so what was the point in trying to play it safe now?

His mother thought that they were involved in something serious, and she was uneasy with that misconception, but they *were* involved and going to Scotland would be…a bit like having a holiday with him. A mini-break.

Of course, he hadn't *planned* it as a mini-break, but still…

She strolled to the window and looked down at the acres upon acres of land that surrounded the country house. It wasn't yet seven and everywhere seemed to breathe with the excitement of a new day dawning.

The helicopter ride had given her a feel for the spectacular natural beauty that belonged to Scotland and a breathtaking first view of Perthshire. Angela had fondly told her that it was nicknamed 'Big Tree Country' and it hadn't been hard to see why.

From above, as the helicopter buzzed and swayed like an angry wasp, all she could see were the rich, varied greens of the verdant forests and rolling, rising hills. There were waterfalls there as well, she had been told, hidden in the depths of the trees, and castles and abbeys and fortresses. It was like looking down at a film set, and she almost expected to see fantastic primeval armies rising up from the undergrowth, surging forward on white stallions, heading for some mythical showdown.

And, over the past five days, it hadn't disappointed. The spaces were vast and open and the scenery was dramatic, shorn of the trappings of civilisation, raw and intensely beautiful. Even the air seemed different, cleaner somehow. London, in comparison, seemed like a tinsel town with too many people chasing too many things that didn't matter very much.

The flooding was in one small wing of the country house and Stefano had taken charge as soon as they had arrived, quizzing the head guy about what was being done, getting in touch with the insurers, bringing in a top chartered surveyor and a team of men who began work almost immediately with ruthless efficiency.

Flora, enchanted by the open spaces, which, she had confided, reminded her of New Zealand, had immersed herself in exploring the woodland, with Angela for company.

'She knows a lot of stuff about plants,' Flora had told Sunny the evening before with a shrug. 'It's interesting. I told her that I could Google all of that on my phone but she said it isn't the same as touching and seeing the real thing. She's going to teach me how to press flowers.'

'Maybe I'll tag along,' Sunny had said, because

Stefano tended to work during the day, making sure that he was in the vicinity to check up on the guys working on the plumbing problems, while Sunny couldn't get her head round doing any work at all, even though she had dutifully brought her laptop computer with her.

So she'd done a bit of exploring of her own. She had started with the house, having obtained full permission from Angela to go wherever she wanted to go. She had gone into every room and gaped and gasped at all of them. It was an old house, dating back to the eighteenth century, but it had been very cleverly modernised so the old blended with the new in seamless perfection. Wood panelling combined with soft grey and taupe...antique fine silk rugs did justice to über-comfortable modern Italian furniture...and the kitchen was a marvel of high-tech modernity, save for the bottle-green double Aga.

'It's huge for just your mother to visit now and again, isn't it?' She now turned to Stefano, who was sprawled on the bed, sheets and blanket half covering his nakedness, leaving just enough on show to remind her of the night before, when they had spent at least a couple of hours languorously making love. They had touched one another everywhere and she quivered as she recalled the feel of his mouth between her legs, nuzzling and licking and exciting, taking her to the limits of a wrenching orgasm, shuddering against his mouth as she had arched up.

Wetness pooled between her legs. She still couldn't credit that she had met someone who could turn her on just by looking at her.

Stefano grinned. After his divorce, he'd made it a rule never to sleep the night with any woman and it surprised him just how comfortable he felt going to sleep with her next to him and waking up with her next to him.

He liked the fact that he could reach out and touch her naked body whenever he wanted, whatever the time of night. He liked cupping her breast, playing with her nipple, hearing her soft little moans as she enjoyed him when she was still half asleep. Her legs would open and it had been hugely arousing a couple of nights previously when he had slipped his finger along her crease to find the little bud of her clitoris and she had come against his hand without really waking up at all, or rather waking up just sufficiently to wriggle close to him, eyes still closed, where she had promptly settled back into deep sleep while he had stroked her hair and her back and her smooth, slender thighs.

'The early morning light is doing incredible things to your body...' he murmured, eyes flaring as they took in the long, supple lines of her naked body.

He'd only just recovered from the surprise of being put in the same room as her by his very traditional parent and he certainly hadn't bought the excuse that all the other rooms still needed to be aired. Like hell they did. His mother had convinced herself that Sunny was *the one* and he had been more than happy to go along with that, thereby saving himself a fruitless conversation denying it, plus having the added bonus of Sunny in his bed without having to resort to night-time subterfuge.

'Do you ever think about anything but sex?' But she was grinning back at him as she turned round to perch against the window ledge, resting her bottom on her hands.

It was cold outside but warm in the bedroom, where the heating was timed to come on for an hour every morning to take the early morning chill out of the air.

'I closed a deal yesterday.' He propped himself

up on one elbow and gazed at her. Her legs were lightly crossed and her pert little breasts were thrust forward in a pose that was innocent and provocative at the same time. 'I thought about the nuts and bolts of that for a while... Come back to bed...it's too early to be up and about...'

'You once let slip that you're *up and about* by six every morning.'

'That was before I discovered the pleasures of staying in bed when the other occupant of the bed happens to be you.' He patted the space next to him and Sunny strolled back towards the bed but she didn't slip under the covers. Instead, she knelt on the bed, hands pressed between her thighs.

'Let's go for an early-morning walk.'

Stefano looked at the enthusiasm on her face and thought how different it was from the cautious expression she had worn when he had first laid eyes on her, which had been way too adult for her age.

She looked...young, carefree. She laughed. She'd confessed to him that when she'd been told to babysit Flora in the office she'd had no idea what to do with a kid because she herself had bypassed all the normal experiences of childhood, and so she'd stuck her in front of some old legal photocopied cases and let her loose, little knowing that her very lack of effort would provide the glue that would cement her relationship with Flora.

'Is it wise for a workaholic to go on early-morning walks?' He pulled her down so that she toppled onto him, soft breasts squashed against his chest, and then he shifted so that he positioned her lengthwise over him.

Sex, Sunny thought. It really was all he thought about when he was with her. They talked, they laughed but, in the end, the only thing that really mattered to him was the touching that they did.

She tried not to dwell on that but, for some reason, it hurt to think about it now and she immediately shoved the thought to the back of her head. This was all about fun and what *wasn't* fun was wasting time analysing the pros and cons of what they were doing.

'Very wise,' she recommended.

'I'll do a trade...' Stefano caressed the smooth skin of her buttocks, gently easing her legs apart so that his erection was pushed hard against her belly. 'Your glorious body and, yes...I'll give you the early morning walk...'

* * *

'So, to get back to your question...' Stefano couldn't remember the last time he had strolled through the woodland that surrounded the country house. Perhaps when he had been a kid, when he'd taken the same pleasure in exploring the woods as his daughter now did, marvelling when he came upon streams and cascading waterfalls.

Actually, he couldn't quite remember when he had taken time out at all... Oh, the odd weekend here and there in the past with a woman, but nothing that had felt as relaxing as these past few days had felt.

He slung his arm over her shoulder. 'Big house for one occasional occupant. You're quite right, of course, and this latest near disaster has finally convinced my mother that the time is right to sell—buy something in the city which she can visit whenever she wants to so that she can keep connected with her friends in the area. Something a lot less high maintenance. She's been reluctant to sell before because not only did she spend her married life here with my father, but the house carries a lot of family history on my father's side. But, at the end of the day, practicality is what matters.'

'Is that why she and Flora are planning on going into Edinburgh for the day?'

'Possibly,' Stefano said drily. 'She claims it's because she wants to treat Flora to lunch in one of the most beautiful cafés in one of the most beautiful cities in the world, but I wouldn't drop dead with shock if she pays a visit to an estate agent. One of her friends owns an agency specialising in upmarket places. She and I have only spoken about this a couple of times but that's been enough to establish that we have very different tastes when it comes to a suitable property for her. I want an apartment. Low maintenance, no land to worry about, no problems with pesky leaks. My mother, on the other hand, would like something, as she calls it, *with character.*'

Sunny laughed. 'That's because she loves this place and probably wants to replicate it but on a much smaller scale.'

Stefano had no need to ask Sunny how she knew how his mother felt about Nevis Manor. She and his mother had clicked. They enjoyed one another's company and, somewhat disconcertingly, Sunny had actually told his mother about her background.

'She asked me about my family,' she had told

Stefano on night number two, 'and I wasn't going to lie to her. It's bad enough that she thinks there's more to us than there actually is without feeding her more half-truths.'

His mother saw Sunny as a candidate for the role of his wife. Maybe she was startled at the choice he had made. Who knew? His long line of transient girlfriends had hardly been intellectually gifted and their charms had certainly never been kept under wraps, hidden beneath faded jeans and old sweats. The mere fact that Sunny was *so different* on every level would have persuaded his mother as to the authenticity of their relationship. Throw his daughter into the mix and you got the perfect scenario.

So she would have been predisposed to love Sunny.

And Sunny? She had told his mother about her painful past and, as he could have told her himself, she had still been accepted, for his mother was anything but one of those shallow snobs who only accepted people according to the elevation of their backgrounds.

Sunny, vulnerable deep inside where no one was allowed to see past the efficient, controlled exterior, would have been predisposed to love his mother for her lack of judgemental criticism.

When you thought about it, it was a match made in Heaven.

But he was not her type, not for any sort of future that was long-term. And she was not his type. Dig a little and you got the soft romantic who really did believe in love, whatever her background and whatever she said to the contrary.

They were having fun and he got a headache when he thought about disappointing his mother eventually with the truth. But by then, he thought, she and Flora would have formed a bond strong enough to withstand the disappearance of the glue that came in the form of Sunny.

He frowned and shoved past the way his mind closed down when he thought about her vanishing out of his life.

'So no mother and no daughter when we get back to the house,' he mused thoughtfully, reverting to the comfort zone that was tried and tested territory. 'I'm beginning to think that I might be inclined to take the entire day off work...'

With the leaks nearly fixed, most of the workmen had left for other jobs and he made sure that the three busily doing the last finishing touches to some copper pipes were firmly engaged in what they were doing and that they had no pressing questions they needed to ask.

'Because I have to work on some important business,' he told them, which made Sunny grin from where she was standing, leaning against the wall, just out of sight, 'and under no circumstances am I to be disturbed.'

There wasn't a workman on the face of the earth who wouldn't have made sure to stay firmly out of sight until otherwise told and, sure enough, they hit the bedroom safe in the knowledge that they were not going to be interrupted.

Morning sex...that would extend to lunchtime sex...and then early afternoon sex...

That was a first for Sunny and she felt heady and decadent when she thought about it.

There had been so many *firsts* with him that she had lost count.

They held hands as they headed up the grand curved staircase and it felt wonderfully intimate. There had been no need to check to see whether his mother and Flora had gone. In fact, they had seen the chauffeur-driven car swing round the bend in the avenue at a little after eight-thirty when they had been returning to the house.

It was easily a two-hour drive to Edinburgh and lunch had been planned.

'The day belongs to us,' Stefano murmured, closing the bedroom door behind them. 'What a shame there are workmen on the grounds or we could have free rein of the house without the inconvenience of having to wear any clothes. Maybe another time.'

'Not if you're planning on selling...' But her heart skipped a treacherous beat because that was possibly the first time he had ever let slip any mention of anything happening at a future date.

'True.' He ushered her towards the bed, bodies shuffling as though they were doing a slow dance to no music.

Had he really told her that he'd bring her back to Nevis Manor? He hadn't even planned on bringing her here the first time! On the other hand, he rather liked playing with images of them strolling round the massive estate and house in nothing but their birthday suits...making love wherever and whenever they chose...

He wondered what it would *feel* like to sit enfolding her in his arms in front of the enormous ancient fireplace in the formal sitting room, in the depth of winter with the snow falling outside and everywhere as silent as an indrawn breath.

He shook his head, clearing it of the fantastical thought.

Instead, he eased her down on the bed, back onto the tangle of sheets they had only just left when they had gone for their early-morning walk.

They made love slowly, taking their time, and then had a bath together in the old-fashioned tub with the clawed feet that could fit them both easily. Without having to surface for anyone or be anywhere, they lingered in there, Sunny quivering as he drew her close to soap her, every last inch of her. Then he towel-dried her, every last inch of her, and undid all the good work by kneeling in front of her, parting her legs and tasting her until she couldn't control the orgasm that left her panting and on fire.

'Breakfast in bed,' he suggested, but stayed her when she would have joined him to make something to bring up to the bedroom. With advance notice, they would have had their usual cook in to prepare meals but his mother, Stefano had told her, had decided that it would be more casual and nicer for Flora if they mucked in and did the cooking themselves, which they had been doing for the past few days.

'You're going to *bring* me breakfast in bed?' Sunny laughed.

'While I'm in the kitchen, I'll make a few calls.'

'So, it's actually about getting a bit of work in,' she teased, reclining on the bed, her vibrant hair spilling over the pillows.

But she still couldn't imagine that he was the type to have ever made breakfast in bed for a woman. Even if he wanted to use the opportunity to slip a few business calls in while the omelette was cooking or the bread was in the toaster... He was making an exception for her and she couldn't staunch the swell of pleasure that gave her.

If she could have bottled the day and sprayed a bit on herself whenever she wanted to feel good then she would have, because the day that passed so quickly was practically perfect.

They drifted into the garden for a picnic lunch, Stefano having dispatched the workmen so that they could have uninterrupted privacy. They shared a bottle of icy-cold white wine and, feeling pleasantly tipsy, Sunny dozed on one of the padded recliners by the pool until she was awakened by Stefano nuzzling her breasts through her

T-shirt and they made love right there, outside, which was another first.

'I'm not sure I can walk a straight line,' she giggled when, at a little after four, they made their way back to the house, dumping the lunch remnants in the kitchen before heading upstairs.

'Lunchtime wine can be a killer.' Stefano grinned.

'In which case, why did you bring the bottle? Did you want me to end up not being able to walk a straight line?'

'You won't need to walk a line, straight or otherwise, when you're in bed with me tonight...' He wished they were having the house to themselves for the remainder of the evening. He'd enjoyed the freedom of wandering around semiclad, knowing that he could reach out and take her whenever he wanted and she, likewise, could do the same.

Their eyes tangled. She was laughing, looking up at him, cheeks flushed, expression drowsy and happy, *unguarded*.

And Stefano felt something sharp tug in the pit of his stomach.

He hadn't signed up for this. In fact, he had made sure to lay down all the rules and regulations that would have warned her against trying to get him to sign up for this. Because what he saw was something he didn't want to see. He didn't want to see that she had fallen in love with him. He didn't want that complication. He'd only ever wanted, from the start, a no-strings-attached affair. It might be an affair with shades of differences to the affairs he usually had, but it was *still an affair*. The *no-strings-attached* aspect was *still* part of the deal.

But her lips were just so damned inviting and, as though recognising some barely visible shift in him, she lowered her eyes and drew back fractionally, although she was still smiling. The unguarded, open expression was no longer there when she looked at him again.

'I should walk my unsteady line to the bathroom and have a shower.' She turned away and began rummaging in a drawer for a change of clothes. 'Your mother and Flora will be back pretty soon,' she threw over her shoulder. 'The last thing I want would be for Flora to come bounding into the bedroom and find me in a state of undress!' She'd opened herself up, allowed him to see what she had barely been aware of thinking herself, and now...

She scarpered into the bathroom and braced herself against the back of the door for a couple of seconds.

When did it happen? When did she go and do the unthinkable? When did she fall in love with him? Was it when he'd been making her laugh? Making her think? When he'd been getting under her skin so that she'd been forced to stretch herself in her outlook on so many things?

She knew it hadn't been when he'd been touching her because touching her, however expert his touch might be, would not have got her here, to this place. Of utter, crushing vulnerability. The very place she had spent her life fighting to steer clear of, the place her mother had spent a lifetime occupying.

She couldn't think of walking away from him without something inside her twisting in pain, and she cravenly wondered whether she had misinterpreted her fleeting impression that a shutter had dropped over his eyes—that he'd *noticed*.

Why would he have noticed anything? she feverishly told herself. Men were notoriously obtuse when it came to interpreting women's emotions. She knew that. She'd read it. It was practically common knowledge. And she wasn't going to test the waters by saying anything. How on earth could she, without declaring her love? Without him knowing just how stupid she'd been?

She just wanted to enjoy him for a little bit longer. They had another day and a half in Scotland. What was wrong in enjoying that small window before she broke it off? Because she would have to break it off. She knew that.

She felt scared. Scared of her own feelings, scared of the way her life had careered off the tracks. The signposts that had guided her all her life had been snatched away and for the first time in her adult life she felt truly lost.

Because he didn't love her.

He didn't love her and he would never love her and he had kept his head firmly screwed on while she had been carelessly losing hers.

She had gone into this with her eyes wide open, believing herself to be invincible because she knew the lie of the land. She couldn't possibly get wrapped up with him because he wasn't the sort of guy she could ever fall for in a million years. He was a being from another planet. He would be her reckless adventure and that would be that. The theories had all been spot on. It was just that Life had stepped in and screwed everything up.

She expected to find him sprawled on the bed, waiting for her, but in fact he was nowhere in the room when she emerged, fully dressed, from the bathroom half an hour later.

Relieved, because it gave her some time to brace herself for when she next faced him, knowing what she now knew, Sunny headed downstairs to find that Angela and Flora were already home. They had become accustomed to gravitating to the kitchen and they were both there, along with an elderly couple and an elegant woman roughly the same age as Angela. Flora sprang to her feet as soon as Sunny walked into the kitchen so that she could regale her with stories about Edinburgh.

In between, she was introduced to the couple and was vaguely aware that they were something to do with the church but that went over her head because the other woman was the estate agent Stefano had jokingly referred to and Sunny was amused to think that his mother had dragged her friend back to the house as moral support in building her case for a house with a garden instead of a functional apartment.

There was tea—cakes that had been bought from 'the best bakery in the world', according to Flora… Sunny was aware of Stefano walking in at some point but she was busy chatting to Eileen, Angela's friend, asking her about the housing market in Scotland and comparing prices to the property in London.

She was aware of the deep, sexy timbre of Stefano's voice, slightly behind her to one side, and when, after an hour or so, Flora yawned, Sunny leaped to her feet and offered to take her off to bed with some warm milk and a sandwich because they had, as she had heard in great detail, had a fancy lunch in the city.

She wasn't aware of the looks exchanged as she headed out of the kitchen twenty minutes later, a drooping Flora holding her hand.

'Darling, if I've disappeared before you come back down,' Angela trilled, 'then I shall see you in the morning!'

Which initiated a round of goodbyes and 'must see you again soon…'

Standing just behind Stefano, who had also turned and was smiling, seemingly as relaxed as could be, she had to fight the urge to run her fingers lovingly through his hair, to kiss the nape of his neck, to feel the press of his warm skin on her lips. She thought that if she were blindfolded, she would have been able to identify him simply by touch, so well had she committed his body to her mind.

His body and everything else. His laughter, the way he frowned when he was thinking and distracted, the way he slowed right down to accommodate his mother, the patience and interest he took in everything Flora did, the lazy teasing in his eyes that could make her feel on the point of combustion.

How was it that she hadn't recognised the signs of love creeping up behind her, like a thief in the night?

How was it that she hadn't thought to question the way she had found herself being sucked into Stefano's life? A temporary babysitter would have shown up, done what she was being paid to do and left. A temporary babysitter, only in it for the money, would have never become involved in his back story, would never have let herself be moved by his daughter. A disinterested babysitter might have fancied him but wouldn't have taken it further.

Sunny could see now that she might be cynical about a lot and might have had to grow up much faster walking a far tougher road than most of her contemporaries, but when it came to love she still had all her illusions intact. She could see now that she would never have felt inclined to sleep with him *just because he was hot*. For her, lust couldn't be disentangled from feelings. Underneath her frank acceptance of their differences and incompatibilities, there had still been something potent and irresistible that had drawn her to him and that something had not been the way he looked.

What a mess.

For once, she was distracted with Flora, only half listening to her childish ramblings about what they had seen in Edinburgh. She had acquired a thirst for castles now and had Googled a list of them she wanted to visit when they returned to England.

Sunny agreed with everything. She knew that *she* wouldn't be visiting any castles with Flora. She had a day and a half left with her little ward and then…

It was ages before the night-time routine was done and dusted. Flora had been overexcited after her day out and not, as she usually was, happy to settle herself with one of her books. She had wanted to talk and so it was late by the time Sunny eventually headed back down to the kitchen for something light to eat before bed.

She had no idea where Stefano was. Usually, he popped up to say goodnight to his daughter, a routine to which Flora was gradually warming, but he had not appeared tonight and she wondered whether he had become embroiled in the deal he had been earlier working on.

She found him in the kitchen and she stilled, standing by the door, because he was drinking.

A bottle of whisky was in front of him and he was sprawled over two chairs, reclining in one with his long legs propped up on another. He slanted his head to look at her and took one long, considering mouthful of whisky and then stared at her over the rim of the glass until she smiled nervously and said something about Flora finally getting to sleep after her exciting day, and wasn't she thrilled about all the castles in Scotland...

'Did you know?' Stefano swirled the glass in his hand and stared absently at the brown liquid before taking another mouthful.

Sunny's heart slowed then picked up a pace. 'Did I know...*what*?'

CHAPTER TEN

'THAT MY MOTHER'S good friend and overseer of many a wedding ceremony was going to be here for a little informal social visit...'

'No,' Sunny stammered. 'How on earth would I have known that?' She didn't know whether to enter the kitchen or turn tail and run so she remained where she was, dithering and hovering in the doorway.

The man looking at her was not the man she had fallen in love with. This man was a stranger with cool, assessing eyes and a shuttered expression that sent chills racing up and down her spine.

'Well, you do seem to know pretty much everything my mother has been getting up to from one day to the next.'

'I didn't ask to come up here, Stefano!' Sunny shot back defensively. She wrapped her arms around her and walked woodenly into the kitchen to perch on the edge of one of the chairs, her body as stiff. 'You've been working during the days and seeing about the flooding situation in the west wing. What was I supposed to do? Hide out in the bedroom and ignore your mother and Flora?'

Stefano flushed darkly. Of course she had a point. But had he banked on her getting so close to his mother in such a short space of time? Had he anticipated that his mother's assumptions would become so indelibly fixed in the space of a few short days? He had known that his mother was seeing what she wanted to see—a relationship in the making that would give him the wife she felt he needed and the mother figure his daughter probably would need in due course.

But the local parish priest's arrival had come as a shock to the system.

He'd understood very quickly that his mother had gone beyond nurturing fond notions about some fairy-tale, happy-ever-after ending for him, with Sunny in the starring role.

She'd started making concrete plans and that wasn't going to do. He'd been lazy and taken what he wanted and there were consequences attached to that—consequences he would have to eliminate immediately.

He recalled that expression on Sunny's face

when she'd looked at him, all flushed and open and drowsily unguarded.

Suddenly restless, he stood up, flexing his stiffened muscles, and scowled down at the empty whisky glass.

The kitchen felt small, oppressive...claustrophobic. He had a very strong urge to hit something—the wall, the granite counter, *anything*.

And he needed to create some physical distance between them because just standing too close to her was an extreme challenge to his willpower and self-control.

'When you left the room with Flora,' he said abruptly, 'I was treated to some not so subtle questions about my intentions towards you.'

'Your intentions?'

'Along the lines of whether I planned on committing to this relationship... Our good parish priest saw fit to wax lyrical on the advantages of marriage.'

Sunny's face was flaming red. Did he think that she had somehow manoeuvred, with his mother, to bring the parish priest to the house so that they could all wage a campaign to get him to commit to her? Was that what he was saying? That his mother had misinterpreted the seriousness of the relationship and she, Sunny, had taken advantage of that to try and wheedle herself into a position he had specifically warned her against?

Anger flared through her in a red-hot wave and she clenched her fists on her lap.

'And you think I had something to do with that?' she queried quietly. The colour had drained from her face and her bright green eyes were blazing with suppressed rage. And he didn't look away. He just carried on staring at her, not backing down one iota with his crazy, misguided assumptions.

Yet why should she be surprised that he had rushed into suspecting the worst of her? He wasn't emotionally invested the way she was. He was in it for the fun and the sex. Sure, they got along, but she suspected that he was the kind of guy who would get along with all the women he slept with. Until he got bored of them or they outstayed their welcome, in which case he would look at them rather like he was looking at her now—coolly, assessingly...with the eyes of a man in retreat.

For a few seconds, Stefano didn't say anything. He knew that there was no option but to pull the plug on this. His mother might be determined that he married but that was not on his agenda and most likely never would be. What was the point of learning curves if you didn't actually learn from them? He didn't have it in him to return the type of emotion a woman like Sunny needed and deserved. He was empty inside.

'Yes,' he said. 'Yes, it did cross my mind because you're in love with me.'

Sunny inhaled sharply. A thousand thoughts rushed through her mind at breakneck speed but she knew that there was no way she could deny the truth of that. There was a certainty in his voice that deprived her of the option of trying to deny what he had said.

'I didn't know your mother would bring Father Leary.' She tilted her chin at a defiant angle and Stefano almost smiled because that just seemed to sum her up. Stubborn, honest, defiant, never walking away from the tricky stuff. She'd fallen in love with him and she hadn't banked on that. Didn't make a difference but he could acknowledge that.

Hell, he'd miss her.

He almost found himself wishing that she'd lied, refuted what he'd said, laughed that laugh of hers and told him that he couldn't have been further from the truth.

He almost found himself wishing that he could have carried on kidding himself that she was as uninvolved emotionally as he was. He looked at her and let the silence gather around them, dense and thick, until she finally sighed and looked away because she didn't want him to see that her eyes had glazed over.

She wasn't going to deny the truth and she wasn't going to pretend that she regretted anything. She didn't.

'I won't apologise,' she said with a little shrug, eyes still firmly averted. She blinked rapidly and took a deep breath before looking him squarely in the face. 'I didn't even think it was a possibility that I could fall for someone like you. You're nothing like the kind of guy I imagined handing my heart to.'

No, that person had been someone like John and she should have put two and two together and realised that John might have been perfect on paper but he had never excited her. Stefano had excited her from the very first second she had laid eyes on him and that had been telling because that spark of physical response, the very spark she had told herself meant nothing, had meant everything. Without it, it didn't matter how much sense a person made, how *theoretically right* they were, it was never going to work because love was so much more than what was *theoretically right*.

'You deserve a guy who can give you what you want.' Stefano felt as though he was swallowing glass but it was the truth. 'That guy isn't me and was never going to be and, for the record, I don't think you had anything to do with the good Father Leary showing up here this evening.'

Sunny thought that this was what was meant by a civilised break-up and she wondered whether this was how it ended up with all his girlfriends. The gentle let-down, the quiet words, the tactful reminder that he'd never promised anything.

Did any of them throw hissy fits?

She wasn't about to do that. The only thing left to her now was her pride and her dignity and she wasn't going to let either of those invaluable assets go.

'Yes, you're right, of course,' she murmured in agreement. 'I do deserve someone who can give me what I want and that guy is out there for me.'

Stefano nodded but the smile felt forced.

'But I don't regret what…what happened between us. I enjoyed it and it opened up a whole new world for me and that was good.' She slapped her thighs and offered him a brittle smile which didn't come close to reaching her eyes. 'I guess this is it.'

'It doesn't have to be,' Stefano heard himself say in a rough, driven undertone.

'What do you mean?'

'I'm not going to be marrying you or anyone else any time soon. I've been burnt once and I won't be stepping too close to the fire again, even if the fire looks harmless.' He had surprised himself because it wasn't his style to try and hold onto anyone. 'But we could carry on…as long as you understand…we could continue to have fun…'

'Until you dump me because you've become bored?' Sunny almost laughed. 'I don't think so. I won't be clinging to you like some desperate, sad woman who can't do any better.'

Stefano flushed darkly. What had possessed him to try and stage an eleventh hour plea bargain? Of course it would be madness to prolong this. It could only end in tears for her.

'Naturally, I'd rather not share a bedroom with

you tonight.' She thought of Angela and Flora and felt a pang of desperate unhappiness because she would see neither of them again.

'You needn't fear that I would make a nuisance of myself but if you're quite adamant about that then it would be no problem for me to get my man to bring the helicopter here early. He could be here within the next hour and a half.'

The termination of their relationship hit her in the gut with the force of a sledgehammer. She nodded mutely and heard herself winding up the torturous conversation, telling him that that would probably be for the best, asking him what he would tell his mother, what he would tell Flora.

Her voice seemed to be coming from a very long way away. Finally, when there seemed to be nothing left to say, she stood up and headed towards the kitchen door.

Some pathetic, desperate part of her wanted him to tell her to stop, wanted him to gather her up in his arms and tell her that he loved her after all.

It didn't happen and she found her feet taking her up to the bedroom, where she packed all her clothes back in her bag and scanned the room to see whether she had left anything.

How could all this passion and love and soaring heights and peaks end like this? With him politely seeing her to the helicopter that, dead on time, arrived an hour later to return her to the outskirts of London, where his driver would be waiting to ferry her back to her house?

It did.

They didn't kiss and Sunny kept herself together and it was the hardest thing she had ever had to do.

She left and it was over.

Stefano stared at the cellphone lying on his desk. Fighting the urge to dial her number was a daily battle he waged, even after two weeks of silence.

It was tiresome enough that he had had to endure a barrage of questions from his mother, accusatory disappointment from his daughter and the unpleasant sensation of being *persona non grata* in his own house.

And what the hell was going on with *her*?

He had to resist the constant temptation to phone the law firm to try and prise information out of Katherine.

He couldn't concentrate, couldn't focus and, for the first time in living memory, seemed unable to move on. The distraction of another woman held zero appeal. It went without saying that he had done the right thing, that there was no way he could continue a relationship knowing that the pressure to return feelings he couldn't possible have would eventually cause what they had to self-implode.

He'd learned lessons from his ex! He just didn't have the ability to feel the sort of high-drama nonsense she would inevitably want from him!

Surely he had made that clear from the beginning? Why, then, had she pushed him to the point of having to make a decision and shut down a situation before it had reached its natural conclusion?

Thoughts churning like angry wasps in his head, he continued to glare at his cellphone and was startled when it buzzed with, as he glanced at it, a call from Katherine, to whom he had given his mobile number for speed of access and as a token courtesy, bearing in mind their mothers were close friends.

Slight hold-up on the job. A technicality in the legal wording that she would have to run past him. She could drop the paperwork round to him on her way home.

'No—' Stefano made up his mind on the spot and felt a shaft of relief that he was about to do something and had an excuse for doing it '—I'll come over right away.'

'It's really not that urgent.'

He heard the astonishment in her voice and swept it aside. True, it wasn't his style to attend to anything personally that wasn't of the highest importance but since when did he have to stick to the rule book?

'I was about to leave the office anyway.' He was already on his feet, moving towards his jacket, which he had slung over the leather sofa in his office. It was not yet five and a Friday. Unthinkable that he would be contemplating leaving his office so early. 'If you're on your way out, just leave it with someone. Leave it with Sunny. I need to see her anyway…I can kill two birds with one stone.'

He hit the underground car park at a fast trot and was in his Ferrari, heading out towards Marshall, Jones and Jones, before he could give himself time to talk himself out of what he was doing.

He cleared his head of all doubts as he impatiently sat in the Friday afternoon traffic moving out of the city, drumming his fingers on the steering wheel, wondering what he would do if Sunny had disappeared for the weekend.

Hunt her down.

There was parking at the offices and he sprinted in, only slowing his pace as he approached the opaque glass doors, and he was his usual formidable, utterly composed self as he was pointed in the direction of Sunny's office at the back of the building.

People were streaming out. The Friday evening stampede of office workers eager to kick-start their weekend.

Stefano noticed none of them. Nor did he notice the interested stares he garnered as he headed in the direction of her office.

Sunny was alone in her office; the documents which Katherine had given her sat on her desk with the power of an unexploded hand grenade.

Katherine had hurried in. 'Stefano's popping in to collect these papers, Sunny, and I've told him that I'll leave them with you. You're not in a desperate rush to leave, are you?'

No, of course she wasn't. Where would she be rushing to? Back to the flat so that she could pick up where she left off every evening? Thinking about him? Replaying memories in her head like a song on a never-ending loop? Pretending that she was getting a grip when she knew she wasn't?

She'd never put in so much overtime as she was now doing because work, at least, was something of a distraction.

And now...

The last thing Stefano would have wanted would have been to see her but she suspected that Katherine, on her way out, had dumped him in a position from which he could hardly backtrack, having suggested that he come to collect the paperwork from the office himself. The thought of him being cornered into seeing her made her break out in a fine film of perspiration.

She had no idea what he had been up to. Had she been replaced? She didn't want to think about that but think about it she did. On an hourly basis. He'd had his narrow escape with her and she had no doubt that he would have launched himself into finding her replacement with an overwhelming sense of relief.

She heard his footsteps approaching and every nerve in her body tensed up as she waited for him to appear in the doorway of the small office she occupied with all the other juniors who had inconveniently taken themselves off for a weekend of fun.

'I have those papers!' Nerves prompted her to rush into headlong speech but, after that outburst, her mouth went dry and she stared at him.

How was it even possible for her to have forgotten just how powerful, how stupendously sexy he was? How could she have downplayed the devastating effect he had on all her senses? He'd come straight from work and, having not seen him formally dressed for a while, she was driven to keep staring, drinking in the long lines of his muscular body, sheathed in perfect hand-made Italian.

Lounging in the doorway, Stefano couldn't believe it had taken him this long to get in touch with her, couldn't believe that he had been stupid enough to have waited until prompted by a third party.

Couldn't believe that he'd been that stupid, full stop.

Couldn't believe he'd been dumb enough to let her go, had been dumb enough to have fallen back on his well-worn creed of being a guy who no longer had emotions to feel.

And now, the way she was thrusting those papers towards him…it was obvious that she couldn't wait for him to be on his way.

'Where's everyone?'

'They've all gone. It's nearly six.' She knew what that said about her and she didn't care. So what if her social life had dried up? It had never been much anyway because she'd been so damned busy getting her foot on the career ladder and actually believing that that was the most important thing in her life.

Stefano shut the door quietly behind him but then remained where he was, back pressed against the door, searching for words that didn't seem to be at his disposal.

Nerves stretched to screaming point, Sunny began busying herself for leaving. Tidying her desk, stacking some papers under a paperweight, taking her time fetching her blazer from the back of her chair—anything to avoid direct eye contact. He hadn't reached for the papers and they were on her desk and she didn't know whether to just leave them there or hand them to him.

'How are your mother and Flora?' she finally

asked to break the tension of the silence stretching between them.

'You're missed. Will you have dinner with me?'

Sunny stilled but didn't look at him. 'I don't think so, Stefano.'

'Please.'

'Why?' She was suddenly angry that he was here, in her space, messing with her head when she should be in the recovery process. 'What for?' she all but yelled. 'I didn't ask you here! You came to get those papers and they're there! On the desk! So why don't you take them and just...leave?'

'I don't want to,' he mumbled, shorn of his natural charm.

'I don't care whether you want to or not!'

'I need to talk to you.'

'What about? We did all the talking we had to do.'

'Do you still...love me?'

'That's not fair,' Sunny wasn't even aware that she had whispered that aloud. The colour had drained from her face and her eyes were huge as she looked at him.

'I've missed you,' was all Stefano could think

to say and her heart skipped a beat, then she was angry all over again for pouncing on crumbs like the needy, clingy, pathetic woman she so desperately didn't want to be.

'You'll get over it,' she said cuttingly, although, deep inside, something flared because did that mean that she hadn't been replaced at top speed?

'I don't think I will,' Stefano muttered, his voice so low that she had to strain to pick up what he had said. He finally pushed himself away from the door, hands shoved deep in his pockets. 'I've been an idiot.'

I should leave... I should just walk out, head held high, because there's no way I'm going to be talked into having some sort of fling... There's no way I'm going to let myself be used by someone because they had the leverage of knowing that I...care...

'What do you mean?' she found herself asking huskily.

'Can we at least sit?' Stefano asked. 'This is pretty hard for me.'

'I'm not going to have an affair with you, Stefano. If that's why you're here...I just can't...'

'I don't want to have an affair with you.'

'Good!' *And it was! Because there was no way she was going to oblige!*

She sat down behind her desk and he dragged a chair over but, instead of sticking it in front of her desk, which would have suited her because it might have given her a jag of much needed confidence to be in the position of interviewer, he positioned it neatly by hers so that their knees were practically touching.

So close that she could breathe in the heady scent of him.

'Then what do you want?' she asked unsteadily.

'I want to marry you.'

Sunny laughed humourlessly. 'If you think that's going to…'

'I mean it,' Stefano stated, deadly serious. He sighed deeply and raked his fingers through his hair. 'After my marriage… I protected myself by shutting down emotionally. It was the safe thing to do. I slept with women but I had no interest in pursuing anything further than that. Sex. A physical act, devoid of all the messy complications of involvement. I'd had involvement, or maybe I should say that I had involvement thrust upon me and I discovered first-hand how disas-

trous it could be. Yes, there were happy mar-
riages but they were few and far between and I
wasn't about to get anywhere near that place ever
again. I was never going to chance it. And then
you came along.'

'I did?' Sunny was hanging on to his every
word and the shoots of hope that had sprung up
the minute he had told her that he'd missed her
were growing thick and fast, sprouting their tendrils into every part of her.

For the first time since he'd entered the room,
Stefano felt as if he could breathe freely. He fum-
bled for her hand and their fingers touched and
held and he tightened his grip.

'You did.' He kissed her knuckles and then
looked at her. 'I fancied the hell out of you,' he
confessed, 'and that was no problem. I could deal
with that. And when I found myself talking to
you, telling you things I'd never told anyone before, I figured it was because you'd entered my
life via a slightly different door...'

'Flora.'

'Flora. You knew her. You'd bonded. It was
natural that you would occupy a slightly different place to all the other lovers I'd had in the
past. And then my mother entered the mix and...

things changed. No, things had changed before then. I just didn't realise it. I didn't recognise that what I felt was no longer something I could control, because what I felt was something that was controlling *me*. When I realised that you loved me,...I couldn't deal with it. I was still clinging to the theory that I was in charge...that I had my parameters and those parameters couldn't be breached.'

'I didn't plan on falling in love with you either,' Sunny admitted on a heartfelt sigh. 'I had my parameters, too.' She smiled at the naive self she had been when she, too, thought that she could control what she felt. 'I fought it, you know.'

'But it was a losing battle. I know, my darling. As it was for me. At least you had the courage to admit what you felt and not back away from it. I didn't. But, hell, I missed you, Sunny. I missed the way you laughed; I missed your honesty and your stubbornness. I missed holding you and waking up next to you and knowing that you'd be right there in bed with me every night. There was nothing I didn't miss.'

'Would you have...come if it hadn't been for those papers?'

'It might have taken a bit longer for me to get

past my pig-headed idiocy but I couldn't have *not* come because I love you. I love you and need you and want you to be by my side for ever.'

Sunny smiled and she found that she couldn't stop. 'Okay,' she teased, 'so you've talked me into dinner after all.'

'Can I talk you into marrying me as well?'

She tilted her head to one side and looked at him consideringly. 'You know what? Yes, my dearest Stefano. I think you can…'

* * * * *

*If you enjoyed this story,
check out these other great reads from
Cathy Williams*

*THE SURPRISE DE ANGELIS BABY
WEARING THE DE ANGELIS RING
THE WEDDING NIGHT DEBT
A PAWN IN THE PLAYBOY'S GAME
BOUND BY THE BILLIONAIRE'S BABY*

Available now!

MILLS & BOON®
Large Print – August 2016

The Sicilian's Stolen Son
Lynne Graham

Seduced into Her Boss's Service
Cathy Williams

The Billionaire's Defiant Acquisition
Sharon Kendrick

One Night to Wedding Vows
Kim Lawrence

Engaged to Her Ravensdale Enemy
Melanie Milburne

A Diamond Deal with the Greek
Maya Blake

Inherited by Ferranti
Kate Hewitt

The Billionaire's Baby Swap
Rebecca Winters

The Wedding Planner's Big Day
Cara Colter

Holiday with the Best Man
Kate Hardy

Tempted by Her Tycoon Boss
Jennie Adams